'Please Miss ... It's a Pirate!'

For Clare, the best Lady Mayoress you could wish for.

'Please Miss ... It's a Pirate!'

Being The Lord Mayor of Newcastle upon Tyne

Peter Thomson

Tyne Bridge Publishing

With thanks to: Bill, Dot, Jan, Jane, Jim, John, Julie, Keith, Sandra, Trevor: staff of the Lord Mayor's Office.

The views contained in this book are entirely personal to the author, and in no way reflect the views of Newcastle City Council.

A catalogue record for this book is available from the British Library.

Published by
City of Newcastle upon Tyne
Education & Libraries Directorate
Newcastle Libraries & information Service
Tyne Bridge Publishing
2001

ISBN 1857951360

Find us on the web:
www.newcastle.gov.uk/ tynebridgepublishing

Printed by Athenaeum Press, Gateshead

Trial Run

It was the drink, I think

I'm not sure that I remember everything accurately. I took no notes at the time, but I seem to recall that it all started in the pub. Looking back I think far too much of my life has been decided in the pub; but that is where it all began. 'Here's your pint; by the way, you know you should think about standing as a Councillor, Peter, you'd be good'. Well I am as susceptible to flattery as the next person, probably more so actually but keep it under your hat, so how could I resist?

Well obviously I couldn't, and three months later I was up in front of the District Labour Party Selection Board being assessed on whether I was a suitable person to represent the Party as an elected member. Amazingly they accepted me and lo and behold, a month or two later, an unexpected vacancy cropped up in a safe Labour seat through a surprise resignation, and I was in. This finally was the end of a period of non-

aligned socialist political activism that had lasted from college days. I had only joined the Labour Party itself in 1982 in the wild and naive delusion that it offered an opportunity for radical and innovative voices access to real power to change things. It was a delusion from which I was to be rapidly disabused. However on 4 May 1984 Peter John Stuart Thomson was duly elected the member for the Elswick Ward of Newcastle City Council.

Elswick was then much the same as it is today – two areas of dog rough poverty, deprivation and social exclusion sandwiching a central area of more genteel middle class poverty. Nobody's rich in Elswick, although the bastards who nicked my wallet from my house a couple of weeks ago are £80 richer than they ought to be. Elswick sits in the inner west end of Newcastle upon Tyne. The four wards making up the inner west can lay claim to being one of the poorest areas in the country. Elswick ranks as number 36 in the table of most deprived wards in England (out of 8,414), and West City, our neighbour, to the east and south, number 40. The other two, Scotswood and Benwell, are at 131 and 183..

Quite how a nice middle-class boy from darkest Surrey ended up representing the poor of the North East is another story for another time. Here I was and here I was to stay through ups and downs, another 13 years of Conservative Government, the Poll Tax, Compulsory Competitive Tendering, this initiative, that programme. For most of those 13 years of Tory government I thought that the problems and difficulties of Local Government were their fault. After four years of Labour I realise it is much more a question of central government versus local government; since Labour's local government policies are in large measure indistinguishable from their predecessors. Anyhow I stuck in on behalf of my constituents and by 1999 I had risen to the top of the list of seniority of members of the City Council. I am next in line to become Sheriff and Deputy Lord Mayor for the City of Newcastle upon Tyne for the year 1999 – 2000, with the almost automatic promotion to Lord Mayor to come the following year.

Different Councils chose their ceremonial heads in different ways, in Newcastle it is a straightforward long service medal. Reach the top of the list of seniority of members and its your turn, simple as that; well almost. Actually there are currently 14 people ahead of me on that list but eight of them have already been Lord Mayor and you can only do it once these days. Another four of that 14 have exercised their choice not to take up the opportunity. The remaining two have the misfortune to represent the wrong political party; well it's not the wrong one for them personally, but it is the wrong one for succeeding to ceremonial office. This is an unfortunate hangover from the days when political control of the City Council was more closely in the balance and the extra, or casting, vote of the Lord Mayor could be vital in determining political control. If the parties were exactly balanced, at 39 seats each, that casting vote would be crucial. Of course it has never happened and is frankly unlikely to. Since the boundary changes of 1974 the Labour Party has had a strong majority that stands in 2001 at 62 out of 78 members. The other 16 are all Liberal Democrats, the Conservative Party having run out of popular support, and seats, in 1995.

Politics is a notoriously fickle business and this balance could change of course. I have to be honest however – this is one of my great failings as a politician, I try to be honest – and say I consider it a sad and mean spirited attitude that denies members of other parties the right to become the Lord Mayor of Newcastle. They have served their communities well for years, 15 to 16 is the 'going rate', and the sooner a generosity of spirit in this matter prevails the better.

Local elections are always held at the beginning of May. Not every Council has elections every year, in Newcastle every 4th year is a break, but they are always held at that time of year. Every Local Authority holds an Annual General Meeting, and usually this decides on who is the Mayor and who is on which committee or, nowadays, the Cabinet. If they do not hold an AGM then every decision of the Council has to be made by all its elected members together. So these AGMs happen from about the 2nd week of May onwards. Newcastle holds it's on the 4th Wednesday of May; and so it was that on 23 May 1999 I was sworn at, no sorry, sworn in, as Sheriff and Deputy Lord Mayor for the coming 12 months.

The title of Sheriff was granted to the town of Newcastle in a charter of 1400 as an integral part of being given County status. It seems that the politics of the time were turbulent. The Percys or Dukes of Northumberland were always a threat to order and stability both regionally and nationally. As England's northernmost region, this is long before the Act of Union, at a time when Scotland and the Scots were fiercely independent, and we bore the brunt of border disputes. Alliances were no doubt made and broken continually and the history of the 'Border Reivers' is a fascinating period lasting through the 13th to the 16th centuries. Backwards and forwards went the warring tribes, raiding, pillaging and generally causing mayhem. The Town Walls of Newcastle were developed for very real practical purposes and several times the town would come under siege. These families or tribes who engaged in these rolling guerilla wars are of course now a large percentage of the 'Great and the Good' of the North East. The Armstrongs, Carrs, Ellisons, Percys, Riddells. Like the origins of most of the British aristocracy they made their names and fortunes through terrorism and theft.

Politics around the turn of the 15th century was just as tricky and cutthroat a business as it is today. Richard II had created Henry Percy the Earl of Northumberland at his coronation in 1377. However 20 years later Henry was in cahoots with Henry Bolingbroke, Duke of Lancaster and Ralph Neville, Earl of Westmorland, who between them ran the north. With Percy help and Neville connivance Lancaster seized the throne and became Henry IV. It was he who gave the Town its charter. Perhaps mindful of the potential power of his recent ally, King Henry made the town a County in its own right, which meant it was no longer under the direct jurisdiction of Henry Percy and thus weakening his power a little.

This was actually a key historical moment in the history of the city. York, Bristol and London were the other towns to be given similar charters at that time. It marked the importance of the town nationally. The slightly curious thing about it was that the castle and its immediate precincts were retained as part of the County of Northumberland and thus the Percys. So for 574 years, from 1400 to 1974 a small area of Northumberland was enclosed by the Town and County (later the City and County) of Newcastle upon Tyne. Indeed the County Hall of Northumberland stood in the grounds of the Castle and is today the Vermont Hotel.

County status, and thus the office of Sheriff was finally abolished as part of local government reforms in 1974 when, for a ridiculously short period of time, the County of Tyne and Wear was established. Ted Heath, the recently retired ex Prime Minister, created it and his much detested (by him, as well as most of the population of the North East) successor, Margaret Thatcher, abolished it. This was an act of almost pure political spite occasioned by Ken Livingstone sticking his tongue out at her across the Thames and some rather sensible public transport policies elsewhere which threatened to make municipal enterprises successful. Actually it's not really clear to me whether the County does still exist or not. We still have a Lord Lieutenant of Tyne and Wear, and a High Sheriff, who were both created in 1974, and it's still a postal address. I do wonder if the present clamour for a regional assembly for the North East would be much diminished if Tyne and Wear County Council were still with us.

So you might be wondering how come we still have a Sheriff in the city if the office was abolished in 1974? Good question. There has for many years been a post of Deputy Lord Mayor; it's a kind of warm up for the main job a year later. In 1996 it was decided to re-instate the title of Sheriff and attach it to the Deputy's job. From what I can gather – already it's a little lost in the mists of time – the idea was to have the post re-instated for the 600th anniversary. This of course was my gig. The charter of 1400 is actually dated 23 May and I was to be Sheriff on the exact date of the anniversary. As things turned out absolutely no one was interested in doing anything to celebrate. I rather think that it had escaped people's reckoning in 1996 that there might be a surfeit of celebration around the millennium that would leave most of us exhausted for further celebrations.

As it became clear nobody was stirring themselves and absolutely nobody appeared interested in marking this fairly significant event, I realised I would have to do something myself. So after a little thought and a little discussion with friends I decided to commission a badge or brooch. I approached a marvellous artist working in the city, Jill Hlalo, and together we planned and created a project to design a brooch to mark the event. This involved children from Canning Street Primary School, in Elswick, where I sit as a school governor. They took part in workshops with Jill and produced their own brooches which we displayed at the Laing Art Gallery. Jill then produced her brooch, which I thought magnificent. It had the shape of a long, thin shield and was decorated with symbols associated with the city such as the castle, the river the bridges and a symbol of new life represented by a tree. Jill, however, was not satisfied, seeing imperfections only apparent to those with fine artistic sensibilities, and promptly made a second version. So there are two of these badges, one in the Laing and one kept with the civic regalia in the Lord Mayor's chambers. At the full Council meeting in April 2000, the nearest meeting date to the 600th anniversary, I formally presented the brooch to the city Council. Thanks to Northern Arts and to Tyne and Wear Museums Service (you see, there is Tyne and Wear still hanging around) for their financial contributions towards it.

Those of you who know the city might be interested to visit the memorial which was presented to celebrate the 500th anniversary of the Shrievalty (that's the posh name for the office of Sheriff). This is the statue of Queen Victoria standing outside the city's Anglican

Cathedral, St Nicholas's. A slightly grander and more public monument than my badge; but then also a damn sight more expensive one. Sir William Haswell Stephenson who commissioned the statue was one of those stonking rich, late Victorian businessmen who made fortunes in many of Britain's industrial towns and cities. He also built and donated two public libraries to the city and the ceremonial chain that is now worn by the Sheriff.

The statue of Victoria stands outside the north wall of the Cathedral facing towards the Central station. This is an ironic positioning according to the story that goes along with its commissioning and production. First of all Sir William ran out of money for a few years, so although envisaged and commissioned for the 500th anniversary it didn't actually get constructed and put into place until 1911, eleven years late. Then they had to decide which way she should face. The old Town Hall of Newcastle used, until 1967, to be a grand old building set between the ancient Groat (or barley) Market and the Cloth Market, facing the Cathedral. So there was a problem. If she faced the symbol of the town she had her back to the church, and vice versa. So they positioned her facing west towards the station. This was fine except for the unfortunate fact that Victoria had a bit of a spat with the city early in her reign when, apparently, she was sent a bill for a short stay she made at the Royal Station Hotel. This was simply not done. In revenge she never set foot in the city again, and it is said that on her frequent rail journeys to Balmoral she drew down the blinds of her carriage as she went through Gateshead and did not open them again until Morpeth. But she was ten years dead when the statue went up so she gazes unblinkingly at the Royal Station Hotel and the station itself which she had refused to look upon again.

I was very keen on the title Sheriff and tried to ensure it was used as the normal form of address. It seemed so much nicer to have your own title rather than being someone's deputy. However, the role of Sheriff is a pretty nominal one. There are relatively few engagements that are specifically for the Sheriff rather than the

Lord Mayor. Most engagements come from a clash or double booking of the Lord Mayor. In these instances the Lord Mayor chooses which of the offers s/he fancies doing and the Sheriff gets the other one.

I found these occasional duties trying. I couldn't really get into the feel of it and, to be blunt, take it seriously. I managed to be late on several occasions, of my many faults this is undoubtedly the most socially unacceptable, which caused the staff considerable irritation. It was only after a bit of a row that I agreed not to wear a pair of shorts to go, officially, to watch the Netherlands National Circus perform. The irony is that the show was part of the 'Relax' Festival, and it was a blazing hot day, and it was in my local park that I am accustomed to visit informally. Sarah, my 15 year old daughter, who served excellently as my Sheriff's Lady (OK, there's the mention darling, will you get on with your studying now) was also involved in this dispute as her attire wasn't judged smart enough either. Well we were relaxed about it all, even if the staff were increasingly uptight. It was at this time that, unbeknownst to me, the office of the Lord Mayor began to compile a dossier on my behaviour, dress and appearance. The trouble with all this ceremonial palaver is that people get extraordinarily hung up about tradition, protocol and etiquette. So hung up in fact that they clearly lose touch with reality. The most hilarious part of this dossier, which I eventually saw a couple of months later, was the tale of the magic tie. The dossier catalogued my inadequacies: 'Sheriff was not wearing a tie', 'Sheriff smoked a cigarette at the wrong time', 'Sheriff's shoes needed polishing', 'Arrived to collect Sheriff at 7.15am Sheriff still in bed' that sort of thing. But in its account of one particular day, my tie, which I promise you remained the same one around my neck all day, was described as being blue, then later in the day red, and then finally it turned green. Always not done up properly of course!

I suppose I should have realised I wasn't going to get away with doing things all my own way but this incident began to focus my mind on just what I might be expected to do and how I might be expected to behave; and on just how far I could go in loosening the bonds of habit, protocol and convention. This was to become, for a time, a major issue of my period in office. And the issue was my red shoes. I was wearing them, actually, on the same day as the magic tie. The event in question was the arrival of HMS Newcastle and the shoes, apparently, attracted considerable attention. They became, within a matter of weeks, a cause celebre. In fact I learnt months later that there was much serious talk about my suitablility to hold a civic office at all if I was going to wear red shoes for the Navy! Sometimes ignorance can be a blessing. If I had realised just how seriously the shoes were being taken I might have felt more nervous about wearing them, which I continued to do from time to time. As it was, it never occurred to me for a moment that any grown-up adult person at the end of the 20th century would seriously work themselves into a lather about the colour of the Sheriff's shoes. But oh dear me they did.

Wishful thinking, a flying start

I have had a great interest in China for many years now, going back in fact to the mid 1970s when I joined the Society for Anglo-Chinese Understanding. I know now that this was in fact a 'front' organisation for the Chinese government but at the time I was genuinely motivated by interest in this huge but largely unknown country. In later years this has been reinforced through a very close friend who studied Chinese, spent a year and a half there in the early 1980s and now works as a translator and has visited several times since. Of all the countries outside Europe, China is the one I am most keen to visit. So I was delighted to find that on my schedule of engagements for 14 September 1999 was a banquet to celebrate the 50th anniversary of the Peoples' Republic to be attended by the Chinese Consul from Manchester, effectively the number two in the UK. Surely this could be an opportunity, maybe to set something up for my mayoral year; I was full of anticipation.

Newcastle has a marvellous Chinese quarter based around Stowell Street in the city centre. The Council put some investment into this area about ten years ago and it looks great; the street lights are shaped like lanterns, even the pillar box and the public telephone box have pagoda style tops to them! Of course most of the Chinese in the city, like I think most Chinese communities in Britain, came principally from Hong Kong. Traditionally therefore there is a tension if not a suspicion between the official representatives of the Chinese Government and the members of local communities. In recent years that tension has eased considerably as

China itself embraces 'people's capitalism' and embarks upon what appears to be a campaign to supply the entire world's cheap manufactured goods. You must have noticed the extraordinary proliferation of such goods marked 'Made in China'.

In the event I made a suitably respectful speech about the achievements of the Peoples' Republic, which actually is not very hard to do because whatever you may think about the country, with its unique, and today increasingly bizarre, version of communism, it has been an extraordinary achievement. In 50 years a backward peasant country, what we would today call a third world country, has transformed itself into a very powerful world power. Of course the population of China is now moving inexorably from being a fifth of the world's people to a quarter. So in some senses it is hardly surprising.

The Consul, who had also made a short speech, congratulated me on my words. Great, I thought. I thanked him for the compliment and went on to tell him how interested I was in the Country. You must visit was his response. I was to learn over the next 18 months that the phrases, 'You must come to my Country/City/Region and visit' and 'Of course you will come to visit us, I will see to it as soon as we return home' and one or two other variants, are uttered with ease. In fact they are very much like the promises of politicians at election time. Politicians do mean what they say to you at elections, they really do. It's just that when the elections are over, and the task of government begun, the grim and harsh reality of delivering all those sincerely held aspirations kicks in and it all gets very difficult. Thus, I suspect, with foreign visitors. They really do want to reciprocate the hospitality they are enjoying, but when they get home and look at the organisation involved it too gets hard.

There's another aspect too. Nearly all the visitors to the city are fairly high powered high fliers in their respective cities or countries. England and Wales (Scotland and Northern Ireland are different) are very unusual in world terms, in having ceremonial leaders of towns and cities, called mayors. The important and powerful politicians are usually the Leader or Deputy Leader. In nearly all other countries Mayors are the publicly elected powerful politicians in office for at least four years. It is, I rather suspect, not until our visitors get home that it fully sinks in that the really nice chap with the chains on, who they insisted must come over on a visit, is in fact completely irrelevant to the business they might be attempting to set up or develop with Newcastle or Tyneside.

Anyway, the invitation never arrived.

That day *did* became remarkable for something completely different. Since 1995 I had been working as the senior employee of a small charity in South Shields. South Tyneside Arts Studio Ltd is a pioneering arts and mental health organisation whose principal operation is an open access workshop-cum-studio in the now redundant and specially converted South Shields synagogue. It was agreed with my Board of Directors that I could have the odd couple of hours off for occasional Sheriff's duties but that generally speaking I could fit in the official engagements around my duties as Chief Officer of the charity. The details of my year as Lord Mayor were yet to be finalised but they were aware that when I succeeded to the Lord Mayoralty it would be pretty much a full time occupation.

So it came as a bit of a surprise to receive a phone call at 4.15 on that afternoon of 14 September from Jane Mossman, the Lord Mayor's Principal Secretary. 'The Lord Mayor has taken a fall in his house. He has been admitted to hospital and certainly won't be able to undertake any duties for the next few weeks. What are you doing at 6a.m. in the morning? – In fact can you get free for the whole day?'

A sharp intake of breath, a moment's pause, and then I asked Clare Gee, my wonderful and unflappable deputy at the time, if she could cover for me the next day. She could. Next phone call was to Clare Satow, to see if she was available to accompany me for the day. She was.

So it came to pass that at 6.30 the following morning Clare and I, and Jane Mossman, were pulling on flying suits and preparing to be helicoptered out from the Gateshead Quayside to the decks of HMS *Newcastle* lying just off Tynemouth. The first helicopter ride for all of us I believe and after the initial slight terror – this is an operational Navy machine not a commercial passenger carrier – I soon got into plotting our course down the Tyne to the sea. This does not take very long actually, being barely nine or ten miles, and before we knew it we were hovering just above the ship and with a neat little flick of the controls plonked down on the aft deck. In fact so short was the flight, only about five minutes, that I asked, politely, whether we could do it again. The shrift I received was as short as the flight itself.

This was one of the very few military events that Clare attended during her time as Assistant Sheriff's Lady and then Lady Mayoress. To stand on the bridge of a large warship as she navigates the Tyne from mouth to Newcastle Quayside is however a real once in a lifetime experience, and it fair to say we both enjoyed it enormously. Clare lives in Bill Quay on the banks of the Tyne on the eastern extremity of the Borough of Gateshead so naturally enough we asked the Captain if he could give her children, friends and neighbours a quick blast on the ship's hooter as we sailed past. He seemed to have some difficulty understanding but after we had asked him five or six times he seemed to follow what we meant. I don't think he was too reluctant. Perhaps it was a bit early, still only about 7.30, perhaps there is some Navy regulation about hooting in rivers, anyway after ordering ear defenders all round we hooted a couple of times and sailed on by.

That was a busy day! In fact it was a busy week. Not only was I picking up all the Lord Mayor engagements but as it happened it was quite a busy week for the Sheriff too and I had to try at meet all the obligations. Off the ship for a pre-arranged radio interview, back for lunch on the ship, cocktail party for the Eldon Square Shopping Centre at 6.30, back to the ship for another cocktail party. A boy could get quite drunk on a schedule like that.

Actually getting drunk can be, potentially, an occupational hazard of the job of Lord Mayor and many a legendary tale abounds of the misdemeanors of one or two of my predecessors. Of course I was not Lord Mayor yet, that is still eight months away, but it soon emerged that I was to be the stand-in for most of the period up to Christmas. In effect I was getting an early practice run. This meant some fancy footwork back at the Arts Studio where I was expected to keep working through that eight months until the following May.

South Tyneside Arts Studio is described in its publicity leaflets as 'A Very Special Place' and so it is. Set up through 1993 and 1994 it opened its doors in November of 1994 and I arrived to run the Company ten months later, in September of 1995. The principal operation, as I outlined, is to run an open access visual arts and crafts workshop facilities for anyone who lives in the Borough of South Tyneside. Not that we ever paid a huge amount of attention to precision geography; if you wanted to come and could get there, we usually did not mind at all where you came from. The 'official' purpose of the Studio was as a mental health 'Care in the Community' resource. It was that hook on which we hung the hat for funders to fill. And it is a very successful resource in that respect, but it was and is a whole lot more than that.

When I arrived funding was thin on the ground and finding charitable trusts to support the proper development and stabilisation of our work was absolutely the main task. To give them their due credit the Social Services department and the Health Authority had made quite a brave gesture in offering some support for a three-year trial period. The trouble was that their money, welcome though it was, only amounted to around half of the bare minimum needed to realise the aspirations and visions we had for the work.

The whole point of the Studio was integration at the point of art-making. That probably sounds like a load of gobbeldy-gook so let me try and explain. Mental illness is a most peculiar disease, most particularly in how it is perceived by other people. First of all there is nothing to see, most illnesses have something to show for them, you look ill in one way or another, but not mental illness. So it is often very hard for others to understand that you are actually ill. 'Why don't you just snap out of it?' is an all too common initial reaction from many people. Of all illnesses it engenders the greatest fear in other people and thus carries an enormous stigma around with it. And yet it is the most common serious illness any of us will contract in our lives. I have used this line with young people many times. Ask them which serious type of disease is most likely to affect the greatest number of them and they will come up with a whole bunch of answers that get it wrong. When you tell them they look at you with amazement. Mental illness is hidden away. Why is it hidden away? Because people are ashamed about it, because it carries a terrible stigma, and because those who are suffering find re-integration into the world, after their period of acute distress, extremely hard.

So now we are beginning to explain the phrase 'integration at the point of art-making'. That is what the Studio does. It opens its doors and offers its facilities and its expert human support to people who want to make art. At the point of making art, in other words when you are inside the Studio, comfortable, with a piece of paper in front of you, a brush in your hand and an idea in your head, everyone in that place is completely equal. Where you have come from does not matter. Where you are going to is only a matter of mild concern. What matters is that you are in an environment where everyone is encouraging and supporting your wish to create. So the integration at the Studio comes from the fact that anyone is welcome but also the fact that about 50 per cent of the members are current users of mental health services.

Just to be absolutely clear about the Studio's work, this is not Art Therapy. That is a different discipline entirely, though it often uses very similar forms of working with art. Art Therapy is a distinctive professional discipline used by the psychiatric system as a form of treatment and analysis of patients. What happens in the Studio may well be therapeutic, in fact it often is staggeringly so, but it is not Art Therapy simply because nobody who works there has any training in that discipline and we are resolutely part of an independent voluntary sector and not part of the psychiatric system.

I am sorry if I appear to be labouring a point here but the views, ideas and opinions of so many members of the Studio are oozing out in my words. You can probably tell how much I cared about the Studio and its well being and development. The question of how to be a stand-in Lord Mayor and keep the Studio moving forward was going to need some thought.

Old friends

Sometimes serendipity, or the fortunate accident of chance, can be wonderfully kind and as I began my stand-in stint some very appropriate duties appeared on the engagement sheets. This, mind you, was after the magic Transit van. You recall that I confessed timekeeping was not my greatest strength and a 7.15am pick-up on a Sunday morning was most definitely not my idea of fun. I had, it is true, managed to get up at 6am to catch the helicopter but that was a very special event. This was the start of the Charlie Bear Cancer Fund Tyneside Bridges Fun Run at the Scotswood Bridge and did not have the same sleep banishing magic. Nevertheless, I did struggle out of bed and we arrived at 7.30 only 5 minutes late to find ... nobody.

Scotswood Bridge at that time on a Sunday morning is a desolate place. We could be fairly certain that we had not missed them, so where were they? At 7.45 a battered old transit van pulled up and out of it spilled, I kid you not, at least 30 runners all kitted out with their run numbers. It was like one of those comedy sketch sequences when you know that just out of shot there is a queue of people climbing into the vehicle so that an apparently endless stream of people climb out. But this was no film trick. They just kept on coming out. Off they went with a quick word of encouragement and we met up an hour and a half later on the central Quayside after they had zigzagged the river. Like so many people who put themselves out in order to help and support charities they were magnificent.

So it is now late September 1999 and I have become, to all intents and purposes, the Lord Mayor of Newcastle upon Tyne some eight months early, and inherited a schedule of events I was never expecting, or expected, to officiate at. But as I said a moment ago some of those were highly appropriate, and that is because they involved people and organisations I was personally familiar with.

The first of these was a reception and lunch for Dame Mavis Grant to celebrate her award of Dameship. Mavis is Head Teacher of Canning Street Primary school in Elswick and the only teacher in a primary school in the country who has been so honoured. You might remember I have already mentioned her school because they were involved in the Sheriff's brooch project where they worked with the artist Jill Hlalo to make their own versions of civic regalia. Mavis had been the head teacher there for around two years having moved, with most of the children and staff, from another local primary school that was merged with Canning Street, where I have been a school governor for the past ten years.

I have already talked about how poor the inner west end of the city is and, as you might expect, this is reflected in educational achievement standards that are – well the best word I can use is *sad*. In the year 2000, according to one of the city's Members of Parliament, there were two secondary schools in the west of the city within the worst 30 secondary schools in the country for GCSE results.

Personally I have always been fond of Mark Twain's epithet: 'I never let school interfere with my education.' Education should be about a whole lot more than scoring highly in Standard Attainment Tests or passing lots of GCSE grades A-C. Rather like animals, children can be trained to jump through hoops, but that doesn't necessarily make them happy, knowledgeable, or well equipped to go out and deal with the world. I do sincerely believe we will look back on our educational policies of the late 1990s and early 2000s, in around 2020, and wonder just how on earth we became so obsessed with producing artificial obstacle courses over which schools and children had to jump or be named failures. I know a number of teachers, who shall of course remain nameless, who agree with this perception and who despair at examination- and target-obsessed politicians who direct educational policy. The reason we have poorer attainment than many comparable advanced European countries is that we spend less money per pupil. You get the education you pay for; it's as simple as that.

The whole situation has now become almost farcical, were it not so tragic. I remember cheating, or trying pretty unsuccessfully to cheat. Lots of us did it at school; it was part of the culture, trying to get away with it. It has been so from time immemorial I suspect. I even suspect that occasional cheating goes on on the part of teachers to ensure a favoured child or two succeeds. But today we experience an entirely new phenomenon: structural cheating by schools to meet OFSTED or government attainment targets. There have in the past few months been several cases reported in the papers of this sad behaviour where Head Teachers have raised a whole year-group's results to meet externally imposed targets – and these are just the ones caught out. I know quite a few teachers, and fiddling an entire year-group's performance figures was absolutely unheard of until now. There is just no point whatsoever in doing this – it is solely a measure of the desperation of Head Teachers to keep their schools competitive within utterly meaningless educational outputs. To misquote Oscar Wilde, current educational management theory knows the educational outputs of everything and the educational value of nothing.

A friend, who is a lot cleverer than I am, says this is the effect of the trickle down of logical positivism on educational management theory. In fact, once he had explained what he meant by this, we agreed that this was the great weakness of much of the current Government's social welfare development, health and regeneration policies as well. Logical positivism is most associated with the philosopher A. J. Ayer, and is an interpretation of the world that says there are 'right' ways of doing things and they can be logically determined. Once this is attached to the flow from the public purse you have a problem. Targets mean points and points mean prizes. This can, and has, led to a climate of obsessive monitoring and evaluation around artificial standards and targets; and to the creation of useless targets which some politician or civil servant thinks are useful but which people dealing with the actual problem know are not. This obsession leads to a partial paralysis of the organisations involved. The flow of resources, usually money, into these areas is controlled by the organisation's ability to meet pre-determined targets and outputs. So disproportionate resources are diverted from the core business, say the education of children, in order to plan activity to meet targets, monitor activity and prove that you have monitored activity. This approach goes right across the board now in health, regeneration, social welfare, training and education. Your attainments are pre-decided and your money dependent upon achievement. An industry has grown up around interpreting and developing these approaches comprising academics, civil servants and consultants – particularly consultants.

One of this summer's *Private Eye* 'Pseuds' Corner' offerings encapsulates the nonsense that this industry creates rather well. From a Department for Education and Skills job advertisement: 'what we want to achieve through the establishment of the Learning Academy is to make learning a dynamic, strategically focussed activity that is integrally aligned to the organic growth of the Department.' Someone must have spent hours thinking that one up, paid for out of our taxes!

Interestingly enough the only area of Government where this does not seem to apply is the Department of Trade and Industry. There they expect to lose three-quarters of the money they invest in grants. No pseudo-scientific management mumbo jumbo there. If they think you have a good idea they give you the money to get on with it.

Nevertheless, whatever I or anyone else thinks about the narrow and limited scope of current assessment criteria, the levels of basic numeracy, literacy and behaviour in this part of the city are significantly poor. The phrase 'socially excluded' is the current buzzword and the inner west of Newcastle has them by the bucketload. Third generation unemployed families are common, and in the gradually declining inner city areas of Britain social disintegration goes hand in hand with a socially induced sense of inadequacy and failure. It just makes depressing sense. If your parents think they have no real value or future they treat you likewise, you behave accordingly, the outside world treats you like a problem, and lo and behold you don't feel you are up to much yourself. The Authorities are the enemy, life is a series of scams and avoiding getting caught.

Against this background Mavis has fought long and hard to offer hope and opportunity to some of the physically and emotionally deprived children in the area. She has done this, at least in part, by recognising that the whole family is a key element of a child's life and that to get results the parents are an important part of the equation. She has been a champion for these poor families and their children and it was only right and proper she should be recognised for her achievements. So too was it right for the city to celebrate that recognition and to add its own by way of the reception. It was a delightful event and good to hear Mavis make it plain that it is the work of many hundreds of teachers and support workers in our schools that deserved this award and she accepted it only symbolically on their behalf.

A couple of days after Mavis's lunch came an event very dear to my heart; the official opening of 'The Cluny'. The Cluny Warehouse in the Ouseburn valley near Byker in the inner east of the city was an empty and disused bonded whisky store – Cluny whisky in fact gave it its name. In 1982 the building was bought by the actor Michael Mould and his brother, also an actor, Roy Marsden. Michael is best known in the North East as the man who founded Bruvvers Theatre Company. The reason the opening of the Cluny was dear to my heart was the fact that in 1975 Michael recruited me, fresh from Drama College. So I owe it to him that I landed in this great city in the first place.

Way back in 1975 we were forging very different ways of making and performing theatre. A collective approach to the creation of material was not an entirely new approach but deliberately devising work for audiences who never crossed the threshold of a theatre, and then taking it out to be performed in the venues those audiences *did* frequent, was. Community centres, clubs, pubs, schools, playgrounds, church halls – we played them all. In particular we were the first professional Theatre Company to develop and promote Theatre In Education work in the region. Now sadly almost entirely disappeared as a theatre form, TIE, as it was known, was a popular feature of school curricula. We took subject matter of direct interest to the school, usually in the field of social, historical or political issues, created a drama around the chosen subject, and then worked with teachers to devise educational development programmes which they could use to carry further the interest and debate our drama had (hopefully) stimulated. In the two years I spent with the company we produced shows on racism, domestic violence, property speculation and developers, housing issues and safety. Invariably we received a positive feedback from teachers who recognised the extraordinary power of theatre to illustrate and explain sometimes quite complex issues. Three of the company, myself included, were trained and qualified as teachers so we understood the needs of both pupils and teachers. The drawback of course was that this form of work was highly labour intensive and as industry, commerce and education have learned over the past 25 years labour equals cost. I don't want to bang on too long and hard about the decline in the opportunities and experiences education now offers, but I do believe we offered insights and exciting approaches to issues which mattered to children, in ways that are now much more rarely available.

The Cluny building was bought by Michael and his brother back in the early 1980s. Michael wanted a permanent base for his theatre company and the building was well large enough for that. So large in fact that Bruvvers did not even take up one of the four floors of the building. This presented a great opportunity to invite like-minded arts groups and organisations to take up some of the spare space at reasonable, affordable rates. Other theatre companies soon took up the offer, as did a number of visual and craft artists who were able to create studio spaces for themselves. A recording studio was set up in the basement by one enterprising chap, and the building began to come to life as an arts resource. It was all basic conditions in those days with the artists and groups having to clear out the rubbish of two decades and try to fix up a habitable working space as best they could. What mattered was that the will and the enthusiasm was there to make something different that met the needs of people marginalised and ignored by mainstream business and arts institutions.

All this was viewed with enormous suspicion by my fellow members of the City Council who represented the area around there, and those parts of the city further east. They instantly dubbed it the 'Loony' Warehouse. An understandable reaction I suppose to something they did not understand and found vaguely threatening, but unfortunate; particularly as 15 years later much the same group of members were happy enough to endorse promotional videos of the city which featured the Cluny. Amazingly it had now transformed itself from the 'Loony Warehouse' into a shining example of an 'innovative cultural business cluster'. It took a lot of hard work, persistence and dedication on behalf of the Co-operative who ran the building to struggle against the complete indifference of the Councillors to their needs for so many years. Thankfully the Council's officers were not quite so narrow-minded and some money was forthcoming for external works to the building; but it was not until the mid 1990s that any proper investment was put in. Millions were being spent during this period on encouraging economic development and business start-ups throughout the city, most of which was indifferently successful and some of which was totally wasted. All the while an idea a good ten years ahead of its time was ignored and rubbished.

Yet another example of life imitating art. That is to say that in my experience artists have often paved the way for society in general to view itself. Take for example the work I have mentioned which the early Bruvvers Company developed in challenging racism and domestic violence in the mid 1970s. We raised these issues probably a good ten years before the nature of prejudice, and the inequalities driving such discrimination and oppression, were even generally recognised let alone effectively challenged. Thus it was with the 'innovative cultural business cluster' which was the Cluny. Not that Michael would ever have used such mangled jargonese to describe what to him and the many others who persevered with its development, saw simply as useful and necessary to meet people's needs.

So here we were, just two weeks into my stand-in Lord Mayorship, and the official opening of the latest phase of development was to be opened – and by me! Serendipity working her magic. This latest phase was a bar-café and performance/function room that had been renovated out of a tatty and unused section of the basement area. I took Clare with me as Sheriff's Lady that evening. Being an artist herself she knew many of the tenants of the complex personally and was absolutely in tune with the ethos that lay behind the development. We arrived and as we walked in received what I think was the only spontaneous round of applause of my whole time as Lord Mayor, stand-in or otherwise. Michael, who it has to be said is a bit of a character, slipped immediately into pantomime mode, some three months early, and asked the assembled gathering to put their hands together to welcome the Sheriff of Nottingham! Oh what a time we had that evening.

What a come down a week later to attend the Co-operative Funeral Service Managers' Conference. I, and perhaps you, did not realise what a huge share of the market the Co-op funeral business has; but it is well over half UK funerals. Their annual national conference was held in one of our posher hotels, the Gosforth Park, which is universally referred to as the Gossy. It was not that bad an occasion but it was, sadly, the venue for the worst sexist joke I have ever heard told in public. It actually really took me aback; I just had not realised that people could even consider telling that sort of joke in public anymore. And no, I am not going to repeat it here. Although I do know an absolutely splendid joke which is the essence of political incorrectness concerning a ferret with no teeth; the point of that one however is that you set it up as being just that, totally incorrect. I am not going to tell you that one either, although a £5 note in the post and a stamped addressed envelope will be rewarded with a version in a sealed plain brown envelope.

Getting down to it

I was now a good three weeks into the stand-in role and the situation of the Lord Mayor was becoming clearer. He would be out of commission until at least the beginning of December and it was necessary for me to clarify my position with my employers.

Running the Arts Studio had been, right from the word go, a hand to mouth existence. My employers had kindly informed me on the second day of my employment that the first task I really needed to deal with was the five figure deficit faced in that financial year (which was nearly half over). Anyway we dealt with that, and scraped through the next four years, and now the financing and support, though not enough, was at least guaranteed. Even in the autumn of 1999, with the Studio becoming recognised and established and beginning to gain a considerable reputation, we were still short of each year's full running costs. Clare and I talked long and hard through the situation and agreed that if I withdrew from nearly all my external commitments to developing good practice and networking in South Tyneside, then we could just about manage to run the business for three months, if I worked an equivalent of a three day week. That is to say, I usually went to work four or five days a week but often only for two or three hours each day. This meant a saving of two fifths of my salary and that saving helped secure the rest of the financial year.

Next was the approach to the Council to ensure I was not penalised financially. Slightly to my surprise, after a check on just how much I would be doing as stand-in, I was granted a special allowance to compensate for the salary loss.

The Town of Newcastle got its name from the Normancastle built by, it is said, one of William the Conqueror's sons, William Rufus, or Robert Curthose, around 1080. This would be just after his half uncle Odo had devastated land between the Tees and the Tweed after the locals had bumped off the newly imposed Bishop of Durham. In the Doomsday Survey the entry against Manor after Manor in the north was 'It is waste'. Chilling stuff.

The first recorded Mayor of Newcastle was Daniel, son of Nicholas, in 1216. This was also the year that another ancient tradition of the Town began to be consolidated; that of the Freemen. It seems that there was a well-established free mercantile community by the early 12th century and by the end of it the leading members had formed themselves into a 'Guild Merchant' which was granted a Charter in 1216. The establishment of what was to become the great city was underway.

The two institutions, the Freemen and the Mayor, were closely interlinked from the 13th through to the 19th centuries. In particular there developed 12 Guilds or 'Trades Unions' representing the interests of different merchants, traders, crafts and manufacturers in the town and they had the right to elect the members of the Corporation of Newcastle and the Mayor and Sheriff. In those days the Mayor and Sheriff were also justices of the peace; so there is an ancient link stretching back through the centuries between the Mayor, Sheriff, Corporation and the Freemen. These links are still ritually and formally recognised and exercised and this is what I found myself engaged upon next.

Down on the Quayside are the 1988 Crown Courts, a building I rather like but which is not to the taste of everyone. Every year, so I was to discover, the Lord Mayor meets with the local judge, the Recorder, and the more senior circuit judges to listen to the reading of the 'Letters Patent'; this short traditional ceremony is accompanied with full pomp and circumstance. The Lord Mayor attends one of the courtrooms in full robes, and the judges are in theirs, with wigs. These 'Letters Patent' are simply the sovereign's permission to hold courts of law and are read in about three minutes. After which we all solemnly troop out again and go for a cup of coffee. All a bit of a pantomime really and god knows how much the judges are being paid per hour to perform it. But here we have British tradition at its finest: glorious, pointless, but somehow disarmingly enjoyable.

A few days later and its off to the Guildhall for the Michaelmas Gild of the Freemen. The links here really are still strong. As I have mentioned, until 1835 the Freemen, though only made up of the 12 ancient guilds, effectively controlled the affairs of the town by controlling the Corporation. The Reform Act of 1835 changed that forever by giving all (male) householders a vote and defining the Wards making up the town and defining how many Councillors each Ward could elect. However the Mayor remained the nominal head of the Gilds, which are held three times a year, and Chair these meetings as well as the Council. These 'Gilds' are a meeting of all the Guilds, or trades, who have received charters which, amongst other rights, give them the right to designate their members as Freemen. The Gilds also serve as the way in which new Freemen can be admitted to the Companies, as the Guilds have become known. This is another marvellous ritual where the aspirant Freeman has to stand with a musket in the one hand and a bible in the other and swear not only to be a good Freeman but also to defend the Mayor and the city.

These Gilds would be nothing but another archaic pantomime were it not for the very special circumstances of the Freemen of Newcastle – their interests in the Town Moor. The Town Moor is unique to Newcastle. An area, today of just under 1,000 acres of open grassland, which sits just to the north and north west of the city centre which, 'from time out of mind', has been used as grazing for animals. It is now a 'green lung' at the heart of the modern city and, though encroached upon over the centuries, cannot be any further developed. The Moor is actually owned by the Council, however its use as grazing for the Freemen's animals is probably pre-Norman Conquest and certainly existed by the 13th century. It has been the subject of many disputes and court cases over the years, as well as Acts of Parliament; the two most important of which were the Town Moor Acts of 1774 and 1988. The 'deal' worked out in 1774 was a classic compromise. Both the Corporation and the Freemen wanted control of the land so in the end neither was granted it. Instead the Freemen have irrevocable rights to graze cattle over the Moor and the Council owns the land, but are constrained to keep it as open land. It was some of the confusing detail around this last point which was cleared up once and for all by the 1988 Act. So how this is interpreted in practice is that the Council own the moor but the freemen have complete rights over the use of the 'herbage' or grass.

Sometimes this does not work entirely to the Council's bene fit. In cases of commercial use of the Moor, such as the Hoppings, or Temperance Festival or Race Week Festival, Newcastle's famous two-week-long summer funfar, all the rental for the fairground rides and carparking charges are split 50-50 after expenses, between the Freemen and the Council. On the other hand, rental for St James's Park, home of Newcastle United, which sits on Town Moor land known as 'intake' land, and the rental for other areas also designated 'intake', is kept by the Freemen for the benefit of the Town Moor Charities Fund.

I was to have a bit of fun with the Freemen in a year's time when Lord Mayor proper; but for the moment I was intrigued to take part in this ancient ritual and the setting is just fantastic. The Guildhall, where the Gilds take place, was built in 1658 and substantially modernised in 1796. Other work has taken place from time to time but in the 19th century a full courtroom was set up there, which remains today. This is now occasionally used for films as it contains large wooden panelled constructions for the judge, jury and defendants to sit in. The dock is still surrounded with the original metal spikes, curving inward towards the defendant, to discourage flight from justice. An appropriate setting for an ancient ritual.

This was to be quite a week of engagements and on the evening of the Gild meeting I was detailed to welcome delegates to the city attending the 'Ageing Pipelines International Conference'. Now you may not have realised, as to be frank neither had I, that the world has so many ageing pipelines, but it does. They are a problem to fix apparently, and they need fixing, or services and resources we have become used to will disappear. I just never bargained for learning so much! This reception was held at Newcastle Discovery Museum which is sited in a building constructed as the headquarters of the North Eastern Co-operative Society. For the past seven years the old courtyard of the building has been the home of *Turbinia*, the first turbine ship in the world, designed and built on Tyneside. It was around this ship that the reception took place, which makes for an unusual setting, but one that works well.

Turbinia, now there is a good story. The first ever turbine driven ship, designed, built and tested on Tyneside and then offered to the Royal Navy who stuck their noses in the air at such new-fangled gimmickry. So what was Charles Parsons, inventor and ship builder to do? Simple, he decided that if the Royal Navy would not come to him, then he was going to them. It so happened that in 1895 there was to be a grand review of the Royal Navy at Spithead on the south coast, at which no lesser person that her majesty Queen Victoria would be reviewing her imperial navy. Around three quarters of the entire British fleet were assembled for the occasion and they were to steam, at full speed in line astern, past the review point where the Queen and other dignitaries were standing. So Mr Parsons quietly brought *Turbinia* up to the point where the ships steamed up to full speed, joined the parade line, and let *Turbinia* go. She went past the pride of the whole British Navy a full ten knots faster than any of them could manage. Oh to have been a fly on the wall listening to the Admirals and Sea Lords trying to explain to Victoria why they had not backed the project.

Within a few years turbines became a standard and much exploited form of ship propulsion not just in the British Navy but in many other Navies and increasingly on merchant ships. Today turbines drive ships and planes; electricity is generated by them, and so on. And it all started here on Tyneside.

The busy week continued with the dedication of a road junction in the name of a Newcastle soldier awarded the Victoria Cross in World War I – Private Wakenshaw – and then to dinner at the Mansion House.

Dinner at the Mansion House was to become a regular feature of life as Lord Mayor but this was only the second occasion, my first where an after dinner speech was required. My first dinner had been three months earlier when, I am sure just to test me, I had been invited to a Defence College event to break bread with a bunch of ambitious soldiers. I had survived this evening without being too offensive to anybody. Fortunately the only person prepared to take me on over the folly of bombing Iraq – which was just beginning to be instigated and, in summer 2001, has still not stopped – was right at the far end of the table.

Dinner on this occasion was to welcome a new Chancellor of Newcastle University the Rt. Hon. Christopher Patten fresh from his exertions in the North of Ireland where he had been compiling the report which proposed the (honourable) end of the Royal Ulster Constabulary and *en route* to becoming a Commissioner of the European Union. Chris came with his wife and three daughters, a remarkable posse of women that clearly set male pulses racing wherever they go.

The University of Newcastle started out as Armstrong College, a college of the University of Durham, offering medical education. It was in fact one of the earliest medical schools in the country with its degree awards going back to 1835. Despite developing a wide range of courses as the 20th century unfolded it remained a part of Durham until as late as 1962 when it finally received its own Charter as a University. For this reason Chris was to be installed the following day as only the third Chancellor. Clare gave me the joke for the after dinner speech here: the first Chancellor was a Duke, the second a Viscount, and the third, well, he was just right on (Rt. Hon.). It seemed to go down well enough, mind you after the booze you get plied with at these events almost anything will go down well.

Chris actually had a great story that I was to use on several subsequent occasions to break the ice and get an early laugh. It is the custom at these events to introduce the guests to the Lord Mayor and principal guest in a formal line-up, and then have a pre-dinner drink and chat. Then, five minutes before dinner is served everyone is herded into a corner of the room where chairs have been set up in order to take the group photograph. This proceeded as normal but as everyone was shuffling themselves into position Chris suddenly rose and told us that he recalled all too vividly Prime Minister Margaret Thatcher's behaviour when the same type of group photograph was been taken of the Cabinet.

'She would leap up,' he said, 'and inspect the troops: Howe, your shoes are undone, Patten, straighten your tie, Hurd, you look a complete mess.' Somehow we could all believe it and clearly she really was the woman of the legends. Chris had obviously had an extraordinary career since being unexpectedly booted out by the voters of Bath in 1992. The last Governor of Hong Kong, of which he has written, and then to the RUC. This was, he said, quite the most difficult job he had ever had to do because the politics were so different. You are in a political world, he explained, where the prime driving force of opinion and political position is not based at all on what you think or believe in. No, it is based on opposing what the other side think and believe in. Before any political group will give you an opinion they want to know what their political opposition think about the issue. It is, he went on, just a little bit like Alice in Wonderland. Except that this is the real world, and as I write, some 18 months after this dinner, the Patten Report is still the subject of much controversy and is yet to be implemented.

The next morning it's off again, to Sage Software who are receiving a visit from the Duke of York. This is not the first Royal visit I have had the misfortune to attend, the Duke of Kent swung by the day after I began my stand-in and I had to traipse around Newcastle after him. I say misfortune not because I bear any particular ill will towards the Royals, indifference would describe my attitude better, but because of the ridiculous palaver of organisation and protocol which accompanies these events. In fact you do not traipse after these people, you have to get everywhere before them, in order to meet them anew at every venue. This involves meticulous planning, to the minute, to allow the greeting party to slip ahead of the Royal in question and speed to the next venue while s/he has a final five minute chat with whoever. Above all, my recollection of these visits is the interminable hanging around waiting. On the lighter side I had made the decision to always wear a 'royal' tie. Its principal motif was white elephants!

The greeting party is quite a performance too. Protocol demands that as soon as a Royal sets foot in Tyne and Wear – it exists at least for Royals – they are greeted by the Lord Lieutenant, followed by the High Sheriff, followed by the Mayor or Lord Mayor of the particular District they have arrived in. So generally speaking I was third in the line-up to shake the Royal paw.

The High Sheriff is another honorary role invariably filled by a rich individual who is well connected. I never did quite work out how you get to be High Sheriff but the three I met certainly filled the description. They, like the Local Authority Mayors, hold office for one year only. People would easily get confused between my title of Sheriff and the High Sheriff. To which I developed a simple answer: 'I am the Sheriff of Newcastle, I am only the 'high' Sheriff in the privacy of my own home'. It used to get a smile; I suppose they didn't believe me!

The Lord Lieutenant is a different kind of ceremonial role entirely. He is appointed as the Queen's representative in every County in England and Wales for a period of time that can be ten years or more. He, and it is always he as I don't think there has ever been a she Lieutenant, also has about six deputies appointed for a longer fixed period than the Mayoral year.

Anyway back to Sage Software. You may or may not have heard of Sage but they have become one of Newcastle's precious assets in the last few years. Started 16 or 17 years ago by a couple of lecturers from the then Newcastle Polytechnic, they have grown to become the largest supplier of financial and accountancy software in Britain and Europe. And we are talking big business here, in the year 2000 Sage became the first Public Limited Company (plc) with its head office in Newcastle to make it on to the Financial Times top one hundred companies; the FTSE top 100. And grown they had, despite taking up two blocks of buildings on their present site they desperately needed more space to expand. Obviously, being a new technology company, it was considered really important to hang onto them. The Council's Chief Executive was out with us on the visit, because we were in the middle of delicate negotiations to keep the company in the city by re-locating them in a new development area to the north west, right next door to Newcastle International Airport. That move has now been secured, and in early 2001 I was to award the company with the Freedom of the city (not that we were trying to bribe them to stay or anything!).

Culture loomed next, and indeed is probably going to loom quite large from now on. First it was off to the Tyneside Irish Centre to take part in the opening celebrations of the Tyneside Irish Festival. There has been a significant Irish population on Tyneside since the 19th century. The usual historical reasons seem to apply here. Huge demand for labour was created by the enormous and rapid expansion of heavy industry and mining on Tyneside from the middle of the 19th century onwards. Back in the Emerald Isle, life was poor and opportunities few, so naturally there was a migration here. The Irish have a strong sense of identity and community that has remained strong over the decades. Perhaps this is something to do with the oppression and suppression of a race or culture creating a perverse reaction of strengthening the identity and the people's determination to hold on to that identity. Certainly that can be said of the Jews, and black Africans sent into slavery, oppression reinforced their sense of who they were.

The Irish Ambassador was in attendance at the Festival opening, which I guess is a measure of the importance of the community here on Tyneside. I exercised the full range of my Gaelic at the end of my brief words of support for the Festival, 'slainte', and a fine hooley we had of the night.

Early the next week it was the turn of Islam when I went to open the Islamic Art and Cultural exhibition in the grounds of the University of Newcastle. Elswick, the ward of the city I represent, has the highest number of minority ethnic residents of any area on Tyneside. Nearly all of them are Moslems and so I, and my fellow Councillors – Nigel Todd and Sajawal Khan, have gained considerable experience and knowledge of the different Islamic communities in our city. Well Sajawal originated from Pakistan so he already knew quite a bit to be fair. What we have, unfortunately, far too much experience of, was all the issues arising out of new communities with different cultural and racial characteristics having to wait some time for the host community to understand them. Racism is a strange beast; I once heard it usefully described as prejudice plus power. Everybody has prejudices (mine is an irrational dislike of Americans) but generally we don't have power over the object of our dislike. A majority ethnic group is in a position to exercise power in a structural way and thus systematic or institutionalised racism is created. I suppose that makes the individual, the 'Alf Garnet' type, simply a prejudiced individual not a racist. Arguments rage back and forth around this one. As a southerner I have experienced on Tyneside a widespread and systematic mild prejudice because of my accent. Now it is systematic and it is prejudice but I can't in all honesty lay claim to feeling I have suffered in a racist way.

What I can say with some certainty, after 17 years representing an area of around 25 per cent minority ethnic population, is that it is knowledge and understanding that absorbs minority communities into majority ones. By and large the most hideous, overt examples of racist attitude and behaviour on Tyneside come from people in areas where there is hardly a single black or Asian person. Ignorance breeds prejudice, discrimination and racism. We received many refugees and asylum seekers into the city during 2000 and 2001 and the greatest trouble seemed to come when they are located in areas with little experience of other races and cultures. In time multi-racial Britain will come to be seen as the norm, perhaps we will even have an understanding of the wheel of history. What goes around comes around, to quote a saying. After 300 years of expansionist empire building that made Britain the wealthy country it was once, the legacy is that we can't just wave those peoples, cultures and histories goodbye.

Pedalling a line

The battle of Trafalgar is associated in most people's minds with Admiral Lord Nelson and 'kiss me Hardy.' However, Nelson snuffed it some time before the battle was over and the command of the British was taken over by Admiral Lord Collingwood who steered the fleet to victory. Collingwood was born on Side in the City of Newcastle, educated at its Royal Grammar School and married in the church of St Nicholas so he can properly be claimed as a son of the city. On 21 October every year he is remembered through a Trafalgar Day service at the Cathedral and a parade of Naval Cadets. His descendants still live in the North East and attend the events. If you are interested, a plaque to the Admiral is positioned just down the hill from Amen Corner next to the Cathedral.

God and the Military exercise a considerable amount of the regular routine of the Lord Mayor and this was going to take some getting used to. During the year, I attended 36 church services and 33 military functions. I am neither a theist nor a natural supporter of military activity but I confess to leaving my time as Lord Mayor with a higher respect for both than when I started (mind, I had started with virtually none for the Military). With regard to the military I guess an early discussion was quite crucial in this respect. It was, I think, on that very first occasion when HMS *Newcastle* made her call. At the obligatory cocktail party, the Navy are extremely good at these things and are obviously granted a generous hospitality budget, I fell into serious conversation about the Gulf War with some officers. A distinction began to emerge that is an important one. In the end I was criticising the politicians who took the decisions to put the Military into that situation. The Military themselves were simply carrying out orders. Now I know that phrase carries an ominous ring to it and I can't say I ended my period of office thinking the Military would be a wonderful career for my children; but I did gain respect, at least, for the professionalism displayed by all the members of the armed forces I met during my time.

For most of my life I have held a dislike of militarism, which I perceive as the armed wing of the material greed of nations. As I indicated above, Britain's wealth, and perhaps her position in the world, was gained at the point of a gun. Indeed our great Tyneside Victorian industrial entrepreneur, William (later Lord) Armstrong, was a great one for ever more efficient killing machines. It is said that the Armstrong's Works in Elswick supplied ammunition to both sides during the Great War of 1914-1919. (Yes, I know it was supposed to be the 1914-1918 war, but the North East regiments were sent off to fight those nasty red Russians directly from France and Flanders, and as a result most of the war memorials you will see in the region commemorate a war that lasted until 1919.) There seems no end to it either. Amongst all the righteous celebrations at the release of Nelson Mandela and the first free elections, which enfranchised all the people of South Africa, did you notice that part of the overall deal was the admission of Armscor to the world's arms manufacturers club? Armscor, in case you were unaware, was the Apartheid regime's arms manufacturer which, because of ever increasing sanctions against Apartheid, was forced to develop totally autonomously and was thus self-sufficient. I was saddened to discover that fact. The argument that it means jobs ought not to be good enough, though I suppose in the desperately fragile post-liberation economy of South Africa they could afford to do no differently. I still found it tragic that one of the greatest liberation struggles for equal rights, peace, and justice of the 20th century had to be compromised in such a way.

Soon after Trafalgar Day is the launch of the British Legion Poppy Appeal and the Lord Mayor not only launches that appeal but, as first citizen, lays the first wreath at the Eldon Square War Memorial on Remembrance Sunday. I had written off Remembrance as a ritual of the militaristic mindset but now I had to come to terms with it as something much more than that. Perhaps this was helped on its way by another event that preceded it.

One of the things you can do, stand-in or proper Lord Mayor, is to invite people to invite you, if you follow my drift. Most of the official engagements are habit or tradition, occasions where the Lord Mayor has become involved and which then just re-appear on the calendar year after year. There is however absolutely nothing to stop you encouraging people to invite you to attend events you yourself wish to support. So it was with the Tyne and Wear Anti Fascist Association who were to hold a candle-lit vigil at Grey's Monument to commemorate the victims of fascism, on the anniversary of Kristallnacht, the night Hitler's supporters started the pogrom against the Jews. Supporting this event came easily and from that I could understand better the route for myself through the maze of Remembrance. I would return to these issues in a year's time when I had developed my views and opinions on the nature of this traditional event, and stronger ideas on where it should be heading.

An excellent dinner, a very large quantity of good red wine, and a recently retired Major General who had just taken over as the national head of the Royal British Legion sparked this off. He had a problem which we discussed that evening. He was now in charge of an organisation run by the will of its members whose average age was over 70. He was interested in the management of change. As it happens so am I and we explored some of his possibilities. It was thinking about all these issues that brought me to realise that Remembrance, an event I had written off as nostalgia for militarism, could and should be transformed in this new century. After all in another ten years, 15 at the most, no one who took active part in the Second World War will be alive anymore. As well as remembering the sacrifices made the whole Remembrance event needs to take on a positive role for the future, and that has to be about working for peace. There was strong disapproval in the air from some quarters a year later on Remembrance Sunday, when Clare and I turned up wearing both the red poppy of remembrance and the white poppy of peace, together in our lapels; but funnily enough, not from a single veteran.

The next day has become important to me, in retrospect, from the point of pure ego. A well known house construction firm had built a block of flats in Jesmond, one of the posher parts of the city, and had invited me to perform an opening ceremony. Because of the closeness to the turn of the year they had decided that this was a millennium development and put up a plaque to commemorate the occasion. I was to unveil it as part of my visit. I was not to know this, but in my proper year to come as Lord Mayor I was only to get to unveil two plaques, and they were both indoors. So this would turn out to be the only outdoor plaque in the city to bear my name. Usually the Lord Mayor gets to unveil quite a few during their time in office but I just lost out to the law of averages I guess; there just were not any that came up during my time. So, mundane though the project was, it has a special place in my heart.

Good news from the Lord Mayor, he was nearly recovered and would be able to resume his duties from the beginning of December. Two further events then, were to bring me almost to the end of my stand-in period. The first of these was to give a presentation to representatives of a large high street bank for their support of the Council's Youth Parliament initiative. The Youth Parliament was a project I gave my enthusiastic support to. Young people have so much to give and yet often feel so ignored and marginalised by us adults. The Parliament, which incidentally keyed in with a national Youth Parliament initiative, was an attempt to say to our young people in the city, 'You have a voice and we will encourage you to find and use that voice.' Two 14-15 year olds were nominated, in varying ways, by each secondary school in the city and brought together to develop a collective voice on issues that interested and concerned them. It was an attempt, fraught with pitfalls, but at least we were making an effort to engage. Whether we, the Council, would listen was another matter entirely.

We did not. There are few more frustrating experiences than being made a promise that is not then kept; and to do that the young people is, in my opinion, the pits. And the Council plummeted pretty near them. At first it seemed to go well. The Parliament spent evenings and weekends together, they were given support to 'bond' as a group with time and space to discuss and debate issues. All of this culminated in a presentation to the full Council in the April just before I became Lord Mayor. It was excellent. Thoughtful, considered and practical issues were raised and a response was promised by the following September. In mid-September I remembered to follow it up. About a dozen officers of the Council should have been engaged in commenting and advising on the suggestions and proposals made by the Parliament. What I found was that the day before the deadline for response to the Parliament one officer had realised that nothing, absolutely nothing, had been done. I made a bit of a fuss. Things got better although I fear, well I know actually, that some of the participants were disillusioned. They got their response of course, but they could see through it straight away for what it was, hurried and incomplete. Later the care taken really did improve and I hope that after a shaky start the Parliament is back on its feet now. I am still taking a keen interest.

The second event was the launch of the 'Eco-Schools' project. I have always had a strong interest in the environment and have supported campaigns against nuclear energy and for a wider and more positive engagement with the environment. Naturally then I was pleased to be invited to launch this programme in which schools would set up and determine their own areas or issues of ecological and environmental concern, and develop projects to address those concerns.

So, about to fade away into the background for six months, I should not finish this section without mention of the project which perhaps, above all others, I will be remembered for. Credit where credit is due and it is due to Clare Satow, my occasional Sheriff's Lady and soon to be Lady Mayoress (although I was still quietly working on that one, little did she know!). Clare, even more than I, was a long standing and committed campaigner for the environment. In fact if she was 15 years or so younger she'd probably be an eco-warrior and live in endangered trees.

It was at her suggestion, around her kitchen table, that the idea of a Lord Mayoral Trickshaw or bicycle rickshaw was born. In fact it soon became known by its proper modern name of Pedicab. Clare had been brought up in India and was familiar with the widespread use of bicycles as an efficient, cheap and environmentally sustainable form of transportation; for goods and people. We both agreed wholeheartedly that the choking up of cities by motor vehicles was getting worse and was unsustainable and had to be challenged. Actually Newcastle and the North East in general has a lower than average level of car ownership, but even so the major roads are beginning to clog up at busy periods. I should really extol this as a virtue of our region, as it really is still a virtue, and I hope we keep it that way. Traffic jams are short and relatively rare outside of rush hour but unless drastic action is taken we will go the way of most other UK cities. So we felt here was a great way of raising an issue and of offering a practical alternative. Not in itself a solution to all transportation issues in the urban environment, but one part of the solution. Healthy, consumes not a gram of fossil fuels, no emissions (save for the effect of those beans at breakfast), and actually a nice, gentle way to see a city.

With some excellent support from cycling enthusiasts in the city, including Jill Hopkirk of the Cycle Centre, Byker, I made contact with a Pedicab manufacturer from Manchester who was happy to truck one up to Newcastle, to use as an example for a launch event which we held in early November. A bit of a risk that, given the climate, but the gods smiled on us, we had a sunny lunchtime, and much to the irritation of several of my colleagues on the Council got first class media coverage including both local TV channels. The Pedicab was well and truly launched. This was two years ago now and time is a healer of wounds, but actually the opposition to the idea within the members of the Council was vehement. Not only was I degrading the dignity of the Office of the Lord Mayor but it wouldn't work, was a silly gimmick, and, absolutely worst of all, was popular with the media and people in general. This was particularly irritating to many of them as I got the credit for it.

The Leader of the Council made it clear to me that I would get no support from him, that he did not approve of the idea and not a penny of Council money would be committed to it. He even had a memo sent round instructing officers that not a second of their time was to be given to helping the project. This unreasonable attitude

pissed me off mainly because my predecessor but one had come up with a delightful but totally impracticable plan to re-introduce a Lord Mayor's Barge to the Tyne (under the banner of job creation). Despite the obvious obstacles, it soon turned out to be completely unrealistic and likely to cost millions to build. The Council spent tens of thousands of pounds in developing and working up a scheme. All of which was simply written off at the end of the day. And they could not find a couple of thousand to support the Pedicab which was simple, practical and, here was the irony, totally in line with the Council's own Cycling Policy. Ah well, that's politicians for you. The cycling policy was one of those tokens to green thinking that are quite easy to write and even easier to do little about in practice.

The motto I was later to adopt for my Mayoral year was 'Newcastle the Resourceful City' and we could be resourceful with our scheme to find and use a Pedicab, and we were.

The real thing

Please, Miss ...

I am sure you are wondering how this book got its name, and if you were not – tough. You can always skip on, or even read something else. The Lord Mayor in full ceremonial outfit is sight to be seen. Fur trimmed red robes (they told me it was fake fur but I never believed them), a jabot (that is a lacy cravat to you and me), the chains of office, white gloves, and, to top it all off, a tricorn hat (a three-cornered jobbie). It looks either rather splendid or slightly ridiculous depending on your point of view, your mood at the time or the phase of the moon. Goodness only knows where all these accoutrements originated from. Red robes seem quite common for Mayors, Sheriffs, Freemen, and so on; the hat is an equally common prop. The only piece of the regalia that can be accurately dated are the chains of office which were forged in 1821 and were commissioned for the coronation of George IV. They appear in both paintings and old photographs and we must assume they have been in regular use since that date.

You do not wear the full regalia on duty very often, in fact 95 per cent of the time you wear just the chains of office. However, visits to schools, and in particular Primary schools with the smaller children, are occasions to air the full kit. So at 9 am on the morning of 15 June 2000, just three weeks after succeeding to the office of Lord Mayor, I was chauffeured up to Gosforth Park First School to attend the school Open Day. I am very fond of children, preferably boiled with a sweet and sour sauce, and the little ones are a delight. They just love the ceremonial gear, which is why we always try and put it on for them. On this particular morning I was brought into the school hall where most, if not all, the children were already assembled. The Head Teacher started straight in with the school assembly service, the children made their contributions, all very much as one expects an assembly to go. After all the contributions had been made the Head then looked around the children and said to them,

'Well children, that was very good, and did you notice that we have a very special guest with us this morning? Does anyone know who it is?'

Quick as a flash a small boy raised his hand with that certainty of someone sure they know the right answer,

'Please Miss, it's a pirate!'

Cue collapse of Lord Mayor, Lord Mayor's driver, half the children, and most of the teachers in hysterical laughter. I think we put him right on who I was, I can't honestly remember, but it certainly made my day and it was a story I repeated a few times; and such an obvious title.

Of course, as I have briefly described in Part 1, the origins of the office of Mayor are ancient and bound up with the rising merchant classes. Roger Thornton, Mayor in

1400, was described some 150 years later as 'the richest merchant that ever was dwelling in Newcastle'. Clearly the Mayors, right through the 15th and 16th centuries, were a whole bunch of extremely powerful and wealthy men who controlled the city's affairs to their own interest. By 1605 they had been granted Admiralty jurisdiction over the Tyne which was to prove to be exceedingly lucrative as sea trade, especially in distributing the fruits of the growing practice of digging up coal, grew and diversified.

You could describe the whole bunch of them as pirates in a sense, as they sought to gain advantage by making up the rules as they went along wherever they could get away with it. After all, they controlled the rules under which trading could take place within the town and gradually extended that control over the staithes on the river. There is some great history there. For a time we fought a running battle for control of sea-borne trade with the Shields – North and South – which sit on either side of the mouth of the river. In the natural harbour of the river mouth is actually where you would expect the trading facilities to develop but, because Newcastle had grown as the large town and the capital of the region, they clearly intended to keep the action to themselves. This was the irony of controlling the trade, the sea-going boats could not physically reach anywhere near the town, they had to anchor in the natural harbour of the river mouth. But Newcastle was not going to let all that valuable merchandise get unloaded anywhere where it could not take the toll dues. Newcastle won, of course, but it led to a slightly bizarre Tyneside tradition: the Keel Men. Keel boats were shallow bottomed and could negotiate the river in its several shallow sections between Newcastle and the sea. So ships would arrive in the Tyne, anchor, and then unload their goods into a fleet of keel boats which would then row up the river to land said goods within the boundaries of the Town of Newcastle. And much the same procedures happened for goods that were exported. Local laws were set up to withhold from other places the right to load ships whilst those keel men busied themselves with the job.

Things got so heavy at one point that in 1553 Newcastle annexed Gateshead. The Corporation of Newcastle actually held on to the ownership of 83 acres of Salt Meadows right into the 20th century, and was still selling Gateshead bits of itself back in 1937. Newcastle also permanently removed from Gateshead the right to hold a fish market.

I dare say a similar tale could be told in many towns, and later cities, across the country. The rising merchant classes saw an opportunity to turn events to their favour and were perfectly ruthless in exploiting any advantages they could from their positions of power. The extent of the wealth of some of these merchants who became important figures is illustrated by one William Jennison, mayor in 1581 and then Member of Parliament for Newcastle in 1584. He had a furnished house in Newcastle, another at Thorpe, and another at Haswell; corn and cattle at Benwell, Woodcroft, Walworth, Norton, Woodham, Thorpe, Haswell and Eden; a warehouse in the Close; a share in the Grand Lease valued at £1,000; leases of coal mines at Cross Moor, Fitburn Moor, Cocken, Newbiggin, and Hollinside; coals lying wrought at 13 pits on the south side of the Tyne; a salt pan at Jarrow; three keels, two lighters; and probably a canny bit else besides.

By the 19th century of course it was the great industrialists who had assumed this role of power brokers in the city. Not all of them were on the Council or indeed became Mayor, but nevertheless they formed an unelected cabal of influence. Just as 100 before them the landed gentry had exploited their ownership of the land to squeeze every last penny of profit out of coal mining by constructing buildings, wagonways, roads, tunnels and so on wherever they pleased; so the Victorians equally did what they needed regardless. Think about it. Who other than the Victorians could have built a main railway line right through the middle of a 785 year old Castle?

Some of the lengths people would go to to maximise their profits were amazing. In the 18th century there had developed a series of tolls on the roads into the town and onto the quayside where trading could take place. As I pointed out, trade was restricted to within the boundaries of the town so there was no choice. The enterprising owner of the colliery at Spital Tongues did the maths and decided it would be cheaper to employ a small army of navvies to dig a tunnel under the town and transport his coal on an underground railway, than to pay the tolls. So that is exactly what he did. The tunnel, known as the Victoria Tunnel, is still in existence and was a major air-raid shelter for the city in the 1939-45 war.

The holders of the office of Mayor and Lord Mayor were by no means all pirates, many undertook outstanding initiatives on behalf of the city and its people; but they nevertheless represent the ruling classes through the centuries and few of them, I suspect, ended up poorer at the end of their period of office.

One more short foray into historical information. You may have noticed that I have jumped about between the 'town' and 'city' of Newcastle and between the Mayor and the Lord Mayor. So, just to clarify, the town was granted the right to call itself a city by Queen Victoria in 1882; and in 1906 Edward VII granted us the right to call the Mayor the Lord Mayor.

Which was what I was about to become.

Peter's Big Day

I had been back at the Arts Studio for five months and now was coming the time to leave the business in the hands of Clare Gee. I was to be retained by the Board for one day a week, acting essentially as a mentor and sounding board for Clare in her stewardship of the Company, but to all intents and purposes I was leaving it behind. I actually wanted to be the Lord Mayor 100 per cent of the time, but having been led to believe I would get loss of earnings compensation I was subsequently shafted by my dear comrades on the Labour Group. So I retained the one day at the Studio because I needed the money. In fact I had already made the decision that at the end of my year as Lord Mayor I would also move on in my work. I told Clare this was a likely scenario, but nobody else knew until Christmas when I formally resigned.

The way the Council works was changing. Important new schemes and developments were being or about to be launched, but the new Cabinet system keeps most members away from decision making until policy has been decided, so like most other Members I awaited their implementation with interest. I certainly planned a few remarks for my inaugural speech.

I have already mentioned that the Council is made up of 78 members, three from each of the 26 wards or districts in the City. Full Council, that's all 78 members, is the supreme body that takes responsibility for the Authority's affairs. In effect though, the 62 Labour members actually run things. That is why the Labour Group is the most powerful body on the Council. It meets privately and decisions taken there are what matter. With such a large majority the real political struggles and divides are usually within the Labour Group. You must have heard the old story about a parliamentary frontbencher who complained that the benches opposite held no fear; it was the benches behind that worried him. That was where he would be stabbed in the back from. I have never held a position of power or responsibility within the Group or, apart from a brief period in the early 1990's, the Council committees. In fact looking round I reckon I am the least rewarded member going. I am extremely proud of this because I attribute it mostly to my independence of thinking and appallingly tactless honesty. In fact I am so unpopular in some Labour Group circles that when the normally automatic nomination of the next Lord Mayor came up at the AGM of the Labour Group, in May 2000, an ex-Lord Mayor actually stood up and said they did not consider me suitable. At the time I made a mental note not to invite him to any official functions as revenge, but sense prevailed and I had far greater satisfaction doing the job moderately well and, right at the end of the year, he accepted my invitation to dinner along with all the other living ex-Lord Mayors. That incidentally was a great meal wonderfully enlivened by a discussion between two lady ex-Lord Mayors as to who was the older. Their combined age was 185.

At my final full Council meeting as Sheriff and Deputy Lord Mayor, in April, the children from Canning Street came in to the Civic Centre and performed, for the half dozen members who had bothered to respond to the invitation, a short piece of theatre about the way the first Sheriff was elected. Then in the main Council meeting I formally presented the Sheriff's Badge to the city to become part of the official regalia. This meeting was the closest to the actual date of the 600th anniversary of the Charter, which was 23 May 1400; the Annual, or Mayor-making, Meeting being deemed already full of enough ceremony.

So the big day, 24 May 2000, approached. The Mayor-making is a real ceremony. First the retiring Lord Mayor calls for nominations for a Lord Mayor for the forthcoming year. There is, as you will recall, only one nomination as a matter of course, although technically others could be made. Then there is a great disrobing and unchaining, a re-robing and a re-chaining, flowers are distributed liberally amongst the Ladies, and the new Lord Mayor gets to make an inaugural address. Finally the new Sheriff and Deputy Lord Mayor is installed, the now ex-Lord Mayor makes a farewell address and then everybody troops off to the Church of St Thomas the Martyr next to the Civic Centre for what is rather touchingly described as 'Divine Service'. Well in my case I did my best to make it as enjoyable as possible, some might call it divine, I could not possibly comment.

It was fun preparing for it. A few weeks before the date I was informed that I had to have a Lord Mayor's Chaplain. I am not a theist, and frankly could have done without it, but orders is orders. I toyed, very briefly, with converting to Rastafarianism so that we could have a celebratory spliff during the service but common sense prevailed and I cast around for the best radical vicar I could find. When I found Jonathon Adams he was great – and a cyclist too.

I had given some indication to the Lord Mayor's Office of the sort of texts, songs, etc I would be happy with. Apparently after I had appointed him Jonathon was invited to attend a meeting with a regular Canon from the Cathedral and the Lord Mayor's Principal Secretary, to discuss the service. He came in to find them tut-tutting over a South African childrens' liberation song, *Unzima Lomthwalo*, I had put forward, which they obviously felt was not right. Jonathon took no prisoners by declaring how delighted he was I had chosen one of his favourite hymns. From that point on we were in the driving seat. I selected a reading for myself from the *I Ching* (Hexagram 48: The Well); my son, Patrick, read a piece from Proverbs Ch4 v20-27 which included delightful political jokes like:

'Put away crooked speech,
and put devious talk far from you.'

And

'Do not swerve to the right or to the left'.

Sarah, my daughter, read 'Lies' by Yevgeny Yevtushenko:

'Telling lies to the young is wrong
Proving to them that lies are true is wrong ...'

And so on in a similar vein.

The children from Canning Street sang *Unzima Lomthwalo* and I put in a 'programme' note reflecting the terrible troubles of the nations of that continent, and how debt repayment makes their poverty worse.

Children from another Primary school, Cowgate Primary, sang two songs written jointly by them and my friend, the renowned Tyneside composer Keith Morris. We finished up with *Jerusalem* which I can happily identify with; and then the grand exit to the final section of Widor's Toccata from the 5th Symphony, which is just fabulous stirring stuff.

Whatever anyone else made of it all I had a wonderful time – probably the only time I will ever organise the content of a church service.

Before we got to the church service I had to make my address to Council which I took terribly seriously and spent, for me, an inordinate amount of time preparing. Well there were a few things I wanted to say.

The city is at an important crossroads in its history as it tries to move successfully into the post-industrial period. It was, I suggested, a challenge it was well able to meet because of its resourcefulness. So that was my theme – 'Newcastle the resourceful City'. History has shown that the city has been capable of changing and adapting itself to meet new national and international demands and priorities.

Quite a lot has changed in the British political landscape in the 16 years since I was first elected. 1984 was the year when a Conservative Government was taking on and beating the miners, bringing to an end 150 years of effective political struggle by Trades

Unions through industrial action. Today a Labour Government is taking advantage of that shift and is proposing major changes in the Local Government landscape. In fact that change was already evident, as the first 'Cabinet' style administration of Newcastle was to be proposed at the second half of the Annual General Meeting.

The introduction of elected Mayors was emerging as a major issue and the Government was obviously going to push them as hard as it could; so first I wanted to make it clear that, in my view, there would always be room for a ceremonial Mayor. I noted the apparent passing of the Conservative Party as an electable organisation in the city, whilst chiding the Liberal Democrats for their inability to form any kind of effective opposition. The Lib Dems, in Newcastle at least, are great. They are so liberal that they clearly cannot bring themselves to insisting that they all agree on the same policies. Which means all sorts of fun can be poked at them in both Council and Committee debates. But this is political point scoring, forgive me. What was clearly of interest to all members of the Council was the role that the full Council meetings were to play. That role was changing and I expressed the hope that it would lead to a renewal of interest and involvement in the Council.

We politicians have a problem of apathy. In Newcastle the turnout for elections to the Council barely reaches 30 per cent. Yet we are running an organisation providing a huge range of essential and useful services with a turnover in excess of £500 million a year. Maybe, after the June 2001 election, we can conclude that Local Government is simply running ahead of National Government in reaping voter indifference. For those of us anoraks heavily engaged in politics this is all a worry. Indeed the changes I mention in the style and form of Local Government that the Labour Government is pursuing, such as elected Mayors, are an attempt to re-invigorate interest and involvement in local politics. Given the huge publicity in the London Mayoral election around the Labour party's choice of candidate and the subsequent the independent candidature of Ken Livingstone, the resulting turnout of 36 per cent does not look like it has made many inroads into the problem. We will have to see if that lack of interest repeats itself around the country over the next couple of years as mayoral ballots take place. They will take place because the Labour Government has passed a terrible piece of sloppy, biased legislation to ensure it.

I don't know what is going to happen, I wish I did. I hope people will find a way to show their concern and involvement in the society in which they live, but perhaps it will gradually take on new and different forms to the ones we are used to. John Kenneth Galbraith wrote an interesting if somewhat depressing book on this subject about ten years ago called *The Culture of Contentment*. His thesis was essentially that most people had most of what they needed in their lives and had begun to lose the need to make political interventions into the wider world, even the minimal intervention of voting every four or five years. This accompanied by a 'street' culture which sees the two main political parties (he is talking about the USA) as almost indistinguishable. A growing number of people might well make the same claim for British politics these days. Perhaps there is a secret shift to anarchist thought; after all they have said for years that whoever you vote for the Government always gets in. Their other famous slogan: 'Don't vote – it only encourages them', seems to be increasingly the order of the day for voters.

These issues will have to be dealt with, in the long term, by future generations and support for young people was the next point I had to make. It is young people who will inherit the mess we leave behind and we, as a Council, were trying on several fronts to encourage them to engage with modern citizenship. Not always with skill, success or conviction as I described earlier with the 'Youth Parliament', which had made its first report to the full Council meeting of April 2000. Nevertheless, we were, and still are, committed to trying.

To reinforce my theme of resourcefulness I had selected four charities, all based in the city, as my Lord Mayoral Charities. Each of them has had to struggle to survive and to deliver their aims and objectives. I have already talked about my role in the early days Bruvvers Theatre Company and I decided to make them a beneficiary. Straight from the speech here is my description of the four:

> Bruvvers Theatre Company has worked for 25 years and more bringing the magic of theatre to non-traditional audiences. Often working at the margins of the arts funding system they have through great determination survived and flourished.
>
> The North East Breast Cancer Awareness Trust have campaigned to raise funds to support women through the trauma of a cancer diagnosis and to raise awareness generally of the importance of regular screening. I was pleased to read just last week of a reduction in the incidence of breast cancer by 30 per cent and that is no doubt in part due to the campaigning of the Trust along with other agencies.
>
> The Elswick Girls Group have worked for over 15 years to provide youth work support to girls and young women in the inner west of the city. They too have often found themselves at the margins of the funding system and again the determination they have shown to provide their services is an enormous tribute to the dedication of committee and workers.
>
> The Trans-Continental Agency is a city based charity who raise both funds and awareness to tackle rural poverty in South Africa. Those of you who join me at the service in St Thomas's a little later will find a South African childrens' song is part of the proceedings. This charity is included because of a personal interest in South Africa and also to symbolically recognise the long and proud tradition of the city in international solidarity.

I was to manage to raise just over £8,000 for them during the course of the following 12 months and what a pleasure it was handing over the cheques.

Finally in my speech I reached the really important part. As I had been describing the challenges facing the city in the long view, 'be like the Popes – think in centuries', was an interesting piece of advice I was once given. I raised the single most important challenge facing any government today, local or national, and that is Agenda 21. In early 2001 Clare and I would jointly initiate a series of public debates on Agenda 21 but in the speech I simply outlined the origin of the Agenda, which was the Earth Summit held in Rio in 1992, and tried to give some life to the idea of subsidiarity which I described as simply 'trust the people'. There is a widespread misapprehension about Agenda 21 which believes it to be only about recycling and the environment. It is about a lot more than that. It actually asks us to ask ourselves questions about every aspect of how we organise our societies. From government to industry to education to culture all of the established structures and forms of organisation should be examined and challenged as to whether they still represent the best and most useful way of achieving their purpose.

Down to business

I am getting into serious politics here and this is probably not what you are reading this book for; well if you are, you may not have got the right book, on the other hand maybe you do have the right book. I don't know. I *am* serious about it but this book is supposed to be about being the Lord Mayor, and for a year I was, by tradition, above politics. Fat chance, as you will see.

After all the ceremony of Mayor-making the evening was spent with a dinner party for friends and colleagues – and my Mum and Dad, who were immensely proud of their son, which was touching to say the least. They still live in Surrey and had travelled up to spend the best part of a week up in Newcastle, their longest ever visit to the city in all the time I have lived here. All the staff in the Lord Mayor's office were wonderful to them and they went away very happy.

Next morning it was down to the serious business of Lord Mayoring with a visit to the Royal Grammar School. The RGS, as it is universally known, was founded in the 16th century during the reign of Henry VIII, but was re-founded as the Free Grammar School in 1600. The Master, Head Master in today's terms, was paid for by the Mayor and Corporation and the original site of the school was close to the building used by the Corporation for its work. Thus a tradition stretches back a long long way that the first official duty of a new Lord Mayor is to visit the school.

I was met by a line of young men in camouflaged battledress carrying sub-machine guns. The Headmaster apologised as I got out of the limo, that this too was a tradition, and would I mind very much inspecting them and telling them how smart they looked. Given that I had already begun the journey of coming to terms with the militaristic side of the job this was no real problem, and they were smart, well turned out and so on, telling them so was no lie. The RGS was an impressive, well run, and fabulously provisioned school. I contrasted it in my mind with the leaky dump my own children attended, a mile away and, frankly, wished I were rich. Apart from a few scholarships, the RGS costs about £7,000 a year to attend. Way out of my league I'm afraid. They are very good neighbours of the state provision of secondary education. The superb new science block for instance is in regular use by children from the state sector on exchange or project schemes.

Of course there is that slight whiff of condescending patronage about the whole thing ... good old Victorian philanthropic values. That is what we are returning to as the concept of state provision, or public provision, is rolled back. What Public Private Partnership actually seems to mean is both the introduction of a profit motive and a return to the concept of philanthropy by those who can afford it, towards supporting those within their society who cannot. Thus the brightest pupils in the state sector are reliant upon access to the private sector to maximise their chances; and schools throughout the city are desperate to find a private sector patron to adopt them. The Private Finance Initiative, which we Councillors are repeatedly told is 'the only game in town' or 'the only well that has water', and other such trying metaphors, is another form of this same drive towards a new form of state provision in partnership with business. The biggest drawback to PFI is that it offers no constructive alternative to the march towards globalisation. Agenda 21 offers a route to question how alternatives could be constructed, which is one of the reasons we were so interested in it. You will gather that I am yet to be convinced by the fiscal policies of the Chancellor of the Exchequer as they impact on Local Authorities.

On to the Vocal Chords 2000 Festival at the Playhouse, a 1960s theatre with a superb wide stage that is excellent for both music and drama. The Festival is run by Folkworks, a broad-based folk music development agency started on Tyneside, which is now one of the most respected folk organisations in the country. There were many old friends singing, organising and in the audience. We do these events well and by the end of the weekend of the Festival thousands of people will have not just watched a great variety of singers from many corners of the world, but will also have taken part in singing themselves. An old mate, Katherine Zesserson, lead us all in a song and even I, renowned for having one of the worst singing voices you have ever heard, joined in.

Saturday brought us to the International Centre For Life for their official opening, performed not by me but by someone far more interesting and famous, Carol Voderman, who was charming as we waited for the demonstrators to be cleared out of the way so we could start. The Centre, as you might gather, is a tad controversial, dealing as it does with the extraordinary and rapidly developing field of genetics. Well in fact the Centre is a mixture of a number of elements all connected with the theme of genetics but what we actually were opening is a visitor attraction.

The centre is one of two millennium projects on Tyneside of which we are extremely proud for no more reason than that they are open, they work, and they do not cost a fortune, either to visit or subsidise. We gaze with a certain amazement at the dire cock-ups in London, which have frankly brought the whole concept of millennium developments into disrepute. Our bridge, which I hope to tell something of later, arrived about on time, fitted its mountings and is now working fine. The International Centre for Life received just five per cent of the funding wasted on the Greenwich Dome, yes that's right just five per cent, and is frankly a roaring success. The detailed finances of visitor attractions are difficult and the Centre's one, simply called 'Life', is actually financially designed to lose a certain amount and to be cross-subsidised by the other elements of the development, which are more closely targeted at the commercial field. However, its first year of trading has seen it exceed visitor targets and it has gained a certain reputation as the exception that proves the rule that millennium schemes are a disaster.

Of course nothing beats the Dome for crassness, but unfortunately a large number, too large a number, of these projects have had what is described as the neutron bomb effect. You might remember the neutron bomb. It seems to have gone a bit quiet these days, but the principle of it was that it was fantastically efficient at exterminating human beings whilst causing relatively little damage to structures or property. Thus the neutron bomb effect of millennium funding, whereby a number of large public spaces of all different descriptions are constructed after which it is discovered that there is no way anyone can afford to staff, run and operate them. Thus they are devoid, also, of the people who would have been expected to visit them. There seems to have been a widespread collective myopia amongst the promoters, consultants, planners and millennium grant giving panels who thought up these projects through the late 1990s that made them create business plans with little relationship to real markets. Perhaps they all got carried away with the craze for market-led decision making without the real experience of real markets. Anyhow, we Geordies are smirking into our Broon (Newcastle Brown Ale – a popular and well known local brew; Broon rhymes with Toon, the popular name for the city centre, and the football team).

The Centre for Life consists of three basic elements: the visitor attraction we were opening, commercial office, retail and entertainment spaces, and a leading edge NHS/University fertility unit. In some ways this latter is the most exciting of the three, being a partnership between research, teaching and patient services in fertility. Genetics, as I noted above, is a controversial area and the Centre has had its critics. In fact it has had two very distinct critics. One was a fellow member of Newcastle City Council, a very powerful and awkward customer who has now moved on to become an MP

(North Durham's loss is our gain as one local wag put it). For ideological reasons, complicated and too long-winded to explain, he set his face against the whole project from the start. As he was Chairman of the Development Committee, and later Cabinet Member for development, this meant his spanner was quite a size and he stuck it in the works as frequently as he could, insisting that it was all going to fail, and that the Council would have to pick up the tab. Well it is nice to see him apparently proved wrong, although a mere year's trading is slender evidence.

The other critics are those who see the evil hand of business lurking behind scientific trailblazing. Their objections centre on the potential mis-use of new discoveries, which they perceive as likely. They have a point and I am certainly of the view that we should guard very carefully indeed the application of genetic understandings. The science is moving faster than the ethics, that is a big part of the issues here. The centre is sensitive to these matters and has set up an ethical project as part of the Centre's work. Known as PEALS (Policy Ethics And Life Sciences), and run by the redoubtable Dr Tom Shakespeare, it acts as the 'conscience' of the Centre according to some, and engages in some genuinely open debates and initiatives. In particular it is concerned that the whole field is not shrouded in scientific mumbo-jumbo but addresses issues, fears, and the curiosity of the non-scientific community of Tyneside.

If you are interested, a good start to finding out more about genetics and the mapping of the 23 pairs of chromosomes that make up the human genome is a book entitled *The Genome* by Matt Ridley. Matt is a scientific journalist and the Chairman of the Centre For Life. He is also the son of Viscount Ridley, from one of the great North East families, and will no doubt become Viscount. The Ridleys pepper the history of the city and the region, with 12 of Matt's ancestors having served as Mayor of Newcastle between 1688 and 1840, most of them incidentally, called Matt.

These grand old families of the region still exert an enormous influence on affairs. The Chairman of Northern Rock plc, the now de-mutualised Building Society, which is another of the precious few large companies whose Head Office is in the city, is Sir John Riddell. The Ridell's have been Mayors eight times from 1510 to 1635. Then there is Len Fenwick who is Chief Executive of the hospitals in the city and Chairman of the Stewards Committee of the Freemen. The Fenwicks weigh in with ten Mayors. Looking through the list of Mayors of the city is a bit like looking at the A-Z of Newcastle; most of the streets are there.

Jolly tars

The Royal Navy are easily the most switched on service in respect of public relations. Or perhaps they simply have the most money. I have not done a count but I sense that I probably attended slightly more cocktail parties and lunches at the Navy's invitation than all the other services' invitations put together. I was even invited onto HMS *Bulldog* (yes there really is an HMS *Bulldog* – I was so disappointed to discover she was not skippered by Captain Jack Middletar). Amongst these freebies was Sea Day.

Driven to HMS *York* for around nine in the morning we, and that means around 50 or 60 selected 'key contacts', were taken out sailing for the day. The other Tyneside Mayors were there, press, industry, the gentry, all the usual suspects I was beginning to feel more and more familiar with as their faces popped up again and again. We put to sea accompanied by HMS *Penzance* and the idea was to zoom around a bit off Tynemouth and show off what the ships could do; which, in its own way, was mighty impressive. *Bulldog* could spin around in virtually her own length and *York,* a class 42 destroyer powered by gas turbines when she is in a hurry, could make a pretty impressive top speed. The plume of water thrown up from the stern at full power rises some 15 or 20 feet above the water, executing a sharp turn at this speed is pretty exciting. They warned us to hold on whilst this manoeuvre took place and it felt necessary as the edge of the deck I was on got nearer and nearer the water.

The missiles these Class 42s carry were described to me. They will be aimed either at aircraft or other ships; occasionally I suppose land targets might be added. They quickly reach a speed of Mach 3, or around 2000-mph and are guided in onto their target by radar guidance systems on board the ship. The idea being that once the ship's radar has locked on to the target it doesn't matter how hard they take evasive action, the missile simply follows them. In the case of aircraft they are detonated about a second before impact so that the 'enemy' plane is literally shredded by small pieces of metal travelling at 2000mph, Ouch! For ship targets detonation is delayed until after it has embedded itself in the 'enemy' and then it explodes.

I cannot help playing the comparison game when it comes to the cost of military expenditure. How many teachers could be employed for a year for the cost of each of those missiles? How many health centres could be built for the cost of replacing one of these ships? This is all paid for by you and me, our taxes, our work to earn the money to pay those taxes.

The next day I was back consuming taxes: lunch on board HMS *York*, and in the evening a cocktail party. Still, at least it did not rain on the Navy. The weekend immediately following was blessed by huge downpours (well it was the middle of summer) and both the East End Riverside Millennium Festival and the Universities Boat Race were washed out. The reception for the Boat Race was in the Malmaison Hotel on the Quayside, generally reckoned to be Newcastle's trendiest, and our disappointments at the cancellation were washed down with an excess of the ever present alcohol. It is a great temptation to drink too much in this job. It is free, it is available, and it is generally pushed upon you (all, as Kenny Everett used to say, in the best possible taste). I know you can say no, and I got better later, but you can understand why there have been a canny few casualties down the years.

Alcohol and Newcastle's Quayside have become synonymous in recent years as the re-development of the Quayside has marched forward. The traditional area for young people to get totally bladdered in the Toon is the Bigg Market. Bigg means barley apparently, so that's appropriate for the beer. The circuit of watering holes around that area remains lively and well patronised and all through the year, come rain or shine, winter or summer, you will see the scantily clad young people moving, often in large groups, from bar to bar. The young Geordie on a night out is a legendary sight and provokes continual amazement amongst visitors. They just cannot believe that so many people can be dressed so lightly when the weather is so cold. It must be something in the local genes.

When the Quayside was being developed, and the bars, clubs and restaurants were springing up, the official line was that we were trying to create a different circuit to the Bigg Market, a more 'up-market' circuit that would complement the Bigg Market but attract a different client group. In fact the distinction is hard to spot. I think the prices are a little higher on the Quayside but that frankly does not seem to make any difference to the determined Geordie drinker. The problem with all this booze driven development is that the grand plans for the area include its re-population and housing development has marched hand in hand with the sprouting bars. We are not talking low cost social housing here; we are talking about flats and apartments that start at £100K + for a one bedroom and a poor view. Now people who pay that much for a location are not over chuffed at the behaviour of the over-bladdered Geordie youth at 11pm. Equally the more up-market restaurants wince at the sight of their customers leaving the premises to be confronted by someone vomiting into an adjacent doorway. Recently the Development Control Committee of the Council, which is our Planning Committee, has been turning down planning applications for change of use to bars and clubs. Appeals are being heard and we await their outcome. There is a lot of money to be made from these bars, especially given the prices – they are almost London prices, and thus vested interests are strong. But then the Council has wider responsibilities than just milking as much money as possible from these interests, and actually there are not many opportunities for making money out of them. That is part of the problem with many of the development issues that face the Council. Yes, we get to have a deciding say a lot of the time, but the enterprises we support, encourage and grant planning permission to do not necessarily deliver a lot back into the Tyneside community and economy. Jobs yes, but all too often the real profits are exported from the region, often to the south of Britain or overseas.

All of this illustrates the difficult role the Council has in managing change and development. We sit, ostensibly, above the grubby dealings of commerce, taking a calm and considered overview, intervening strategically to control the greed and ambition of businesses in the wider interest of the long-term benefit of the city and its people. Well that is the theory, but the practice ain't so simple.

Deals are what the world is about and deals are something the Council has been getting itself involved in for a long time. I bet there were some really fascinating deals around the time that the railway line was driven through the middle of the Castle. Many of my predecessors, as I have already suggested, would have been right in the thick of any deals going in their day. Today the Lord Mayor is a symbolic, ceremonial office, and those kinds of deals are the province of the democratically elected Council leadership, or are supposed to be. Cynics suggest that it is often powerful Chief Officers who actually drive these agendas. One ex-Leader of the Council, T. Dan Smith, is probably well remembered by many people throughout Britain, and largely for the wrong reasons, but that is another story. Far fewer will remember Wilf Burns who, as Head of Planning in the city, was at least as responsible as Dan was for the transformation of the city centre in the 1960s.

Today the Chief Officers, and in particular the Chief Executive, of any major city is a powerful local figure. In Newcastle's case he (there *are* women Chief Executives) is the senior employee of a business turning over half a billion pounds a year, which makes it one of the largest businesses in the city. The politicians can be regarded as only figureheads of these businesses but for god's sake don't tell them that, as their egos would never recover. Perhaps there is a clue here to the voter apathy I discussed earlier. Perhaps the people are a bit cleverer than they are often given credit for and, recognising that the people who really run the city are not the ones up for election, reckon their vote unimportant or, worse, irrelevant.

Anyway the Quayside gives, I think, a very good example of the conflicts of interest Councils have to reconcile; and they often get it wrong in part.

Talking of getting it wrong in part, we were off to the Dome. It was not a good day. I have already said nearly enough about the Dome anyway, but to add to the general lack of enthusiasm for the trip I was suffering from Lady Mayoressoral displeasure as a result of my over-indulgence at the Malmaison the day before.

Every Education Authority in England and Wales had been invited by one of the Dome's main sponsors, Macdonald's, to create a performance piece about their town or area. The local dignitaries were then invited, along with those children and adults chosen to perform, to spend a day in the Dome. The devised piece was performed two or three times during the course of the day. The dignitaries of course got a slap up meal courtesy of Ronald Macdonald. Curiously enough they did not serve us burgers and fries washed down with a regular coke, but a rather nice meal with a choice of fine wine. In Newcastle we have a Regional Dance Development Agency called Dance City and it was they who had taken on the task of producing Newcastle's performance piece. I may not have had a very good day, the Dome might be a scandalous and monumental folly of homage to a misplaced echo of a grand imperialist past, but the performance of the group of adults and children put on in the name of the City of Newcastle was cracking good. I was well proud of them.

The Dome was, well it was big; but at least we had the foresight to book a 'flight' on the London Eye in the mid-afternoon which meant we could escape fairly quickly. The Eye was a treat even though we had mediocre weather and poor visibility. A bit scary at first I must confess, I found the way the glass wrapped around towards the floor just a tad disconcerting, but I soon overcame that fear and enjoyed it. As you get older your head for heights seems to diminish I have found. Twenty years ago I would have loved to go hang gliding, now I would not even consider it. To finish the day I was invited to a reception to help the development of our European City of Culture 2008 bid. This was linked to a performance of a play called *Cooking With Elvis* written by Newcastle writer Lee Hall and first produced on Tyneside by the Live Theatre Company at their Quayside premises The Live Theatre. So successful had this production been that it had achieved a West End transfer and was now playing the Whitehall Theatre, for so many years the home of Brian Rix farces. The play is a modern light comedy of sexual manners and great fun. Fortunately we had Trevor Fox playing the 'star' role instead of the actual star, Frank Skinner. Nothing against Frank who I am sure made a good fist of it but Trevor is a Geordie, the part is for a Geordie, and he was riotously, funny.

Running into trouble

Ah went t' Blaydon Races 'twas on the 9th of June
Eighteen hundred an' sixty three on a summas afternoon
We took the Bus fra Balmbra's and she was heavy laden
Awa we went doon Collingwood Street that's on the road t' Blaydon.

So starts probably the best known and most popular of all Geordie songs celebrating a rare day off from the pits or the shipyards, when the population of the Toon went racing. About 15 years ago the local Blaydon Harriers and Athletic Club decided to instigate a running race from Collingwood Street, a few yards from Balmbra's pub, to the site of the racecourse at Blaydon, on 9 of June, as described in the song. The distance is about seven miles and the race has now become a popular fun run, as well as continuing to be a top class trial for élite athletes. It is not quite in the same league as the Great North Run in terms of running stars and popular participation, but it is popular.

The Lord Mayor is usually expected to start the race by ringing a bell. The bell is the original Town Crier of Blaydon's bell, which is mentioned in the song itself. It is a moderate sized hand bell, which does not seem too heavy, at first. However even a modest couple of thousand people take quite a few minutes to reach and pass the start point and, long before they are all through a peculiar phenomena takes place, the bell seems to stop working properly. Now you have been warned that you are expected to ring every runner past you, and you can see, out of the corner of your eye, that they still stretch back miles. You want to ring every runner past you but it is rapidly becoming impossible to get it to strike. It is a difficult moment. I finally sussed it. As you ring the bell, very slowly but gradually, the clanger rotates on its screw thread and loosens. At a certain point the physical dynamics lead it to start to roll around the inside of the bell rather than swinging free and hitting the sides. So a technique has to be quickly improvised to screw the clanger back whilst still giving regular rings. It takes about six or seven minutes for them all to pass you, and with all the ringing and screwing back the clanger and ringing again, by the end you need a rest.

The Great North Run is the region's most famous running event and I had committed myself to taking part this year in order to raise money for my four charities. As I said in the programme notes for the Blaydon Race, in which both the Mayors of both Gateshead and Newcastle are invited to make encouraging remarks, I hated running. I was in training twice a week by this time, most weeks at least, and struggling to manage three miles. I had a long way to go, but at least it was to be run in October this year rather than the usual September, so a vital extra four weeks were available to me. The GNR is a half marathon, a little over 13 miles, and a much more serious prospect than the Blaydon Race. It is in its 17th year now and I was invited to the launch party at the BBC. This was notable principally for the story of the runners' kit in the first ever race. It must have seemed logical to someone at the time but; they offered every runner free transportation of their clothes to the finish line and black plastic bags were distributed at the start. That was it, just black plastic bags. They were all thrown into the back of two lorries, as there were only a couple of thousand runners, it being the first ever run, and the lorries driven to South Shields. Nobody had thought of labels. As the runners arrived they must have contemplated the 2,000 black plastic bags and wondered what on earth had possessed them to give up their clothes in the first place.

Running appears to act like a drug to some people. Devotees become quite obsessed with the smallest and apparently trivial factors that might affect their performance. Above all, the desire to fill as much as possible of your time with running would seem to overwhelm them. They seem invariably to be carrying an injury, preferably two, one of which recurs according to mysterious circumstances that no-one can predict or define; and always returns at a crucial point in the re-habilitation programme of another injury.

I was not a drug addict for running. So why did I do it? This was a question I asked myself not infrequently in the months between April and September of that year. As I had openly admitted I hated it and, when I thought about it, I figured I had not run further than half a mile in one go for at least 25 years. When you run two really unpleasant things tend to happen. First you get out of breath, second your legs start to hurt. By running slowly I did eventually get over the first of these but I never conquered the second.

There is, I think, no doubt that I must have been drunk at the time I made, or at least announced, the decision. Alcohol makes problems go away, seem unimportant, something easily dealt with. I suppose the real reasons, like so much of our decisions in life, came down to ego. Well I had said I was going to do it so I could not back down could I? Clare was keen and made it perfectly clear that the potential benefit to my waistline was a factor I should take seriously. I had to agree, reluctantly, to this proposition. I was 48 years old now and, well let's not put too fine a point on it, I was thickening up. Once I was a 30 inch waist, in fact I was a 30 for ages it seems; a golden age of me perhaps. Then it was 32, then 34, now I was knocking hard on the door of 36. I also, secretly, wanted to see if I could do it. It was a challenge that, after all, thousands of people managed to do every year, quite a few of them as ancient and podgy as me. Then there was the fact that as the first ever Lord Mayor of Newcastle to do the run in office it would gain a good deal of publicity and presented me with a heaven sent opportunity to raise far more sponsorship for my charities than I would ever have again.

So that is why you could find me at the West End Health Resources Centre in Benwell, in the gym, of an early morning; or pounding the footpaths of Hebburn Riverside Country Park having been thrown out of Clare's with the instructions to run if I wanted breakfast. Later I took to running around the Town Moor, twice round, I seem to remember, towards the end of the training. I do not look back on it now with any affection. No rosy glow of nostalgia sweeps over me calling me back to the pavements and paths. In the end I managed runs of perhaps ten or 11 miles in my final two weeks of training. It is true, in fact, that by this point I was finding a certain meditative pleasure in these hour and a half sessions of doing nothing other than pad steadily down pavements and along footpaths. That was it, mind; and was not this pleasure the same as one gets just being alone with your thoughts and no distractions? This is a rare activity for many people in the rush and turmoil of modern living. Unless you run or meditate it is an unusual experience for most of us.

The morning of the Great North Run itself dawned perfectly. Cool but clear and sunny most of the morning (I am afraid I can't remember the afternoon). This Millennium Year run was the largest ever at over 50,000 entries. A year before, during my stand-in period, I had, as is now traditional, started the wheelchair race. The two local football managers, Peter Reid from Sunderland and the newly appointed Bobby Robson from Newcastle, were the star attractions that year, starting the main race. That was amusing largely for the frantic manoeuvring of the runners into the correct side of the start podium. You see Peter Reid of Sunderland was on one side of the podium sited in the central reservation of the inner city motorway, and Bobby Robson was on the other. Black and white shirted runners streaming one way as the red and whites pushed the other, each desperate to change carriageway. If you are unaware of the rivalry between the two sets of supporters – no rivalry is too inadequate a word, genetically encoded hatred is a better description – then you will not fully appreciate the sight I witnessed. I find it hard to understand but I am not a born Geordie, for some of those who are the dislike seems pretty deep down. I know of two cases of men, this is absolutely true, who refused, point blank, to ever use the postal address Tyne and Wear because it contained the word Wear. Such is football rivalry in the North East.

Today there is a universally popular star to send the main race on its way – Jonathon Edwards the Olympic triple jump champion who we had honoured with a luncheon at the Mansion House a few weeks earlier. He is exactly the charming and very caring man the media portray him as, and it was a real pleasure to see him again. He is also, a bit like Clare and myself, a living embodiment of the Newcastle Gateshead partnership which, during 2000, was beginning to gain a real momentum. Whereas Clare lives in Gateshead and I in Newcastle, Jonathon combines the two himself, being a Newcastle resident but a Gateshead Harrier, training at the

Gateshead International Stadium.

I ran to South Shields, stopping only to give a television interview as they had designated me a 'celebrity runner'. Fortunately this was at only six miles in and I still retained my composure and breath. It was a marvellous opportunity to plug not just the event and the North East's ability to stage world class activities, which we do well, but also to give a special plug for our joint bid with Gateshead for the title of European City of Culture 2008. Live national television opportunities are few and far between so I was pleased with myself for taking it. The pleasure soon wore off. I had not run 13 miles before, I shall never do it again – certainly not in the Great North Run, but we will come to that, and the last two miles was an agony and discomfort I believe I will never forget. My son, Patrick (17 years old, six feet two inches tall, rugby player, fit as a butcher's dog), had gallantly agreed to be my support runner and keep me going. He found it completely impossible to run as slowly as I and had to keep stopping to let me catch up. Bless him, he stuck with me all the way despite obvious frustration and we finished together. Within three minutes I was unable to walk normally and this state persisted for the next two days. At least I was able to smoke a tab (that's Geordie for a fag) and drink a bottle of Broon Ale when I arrived, so there was some relief from the apparent paralysis below my hips.

The Great North Run is an incredible event. In 2000 over 35,000 people finished the run out of over 50,000 starters; and even in normal years there are usually 25,000 finishers from 35,000 starters. A huge number of runners take a lot of time and effort, on top of their training, to collect sponsorship for charities of their choice. A lot of money is raised in this way. Just take a pretty conservative estimate. If 30,000 runners each raise £50, which is a modest amount, then £1.5M goes to charities. Not surprisingly the whole event is largely regarded as a charity run, but it is not. Sadly my experience was to end on a sour note.

When, in early December, an invitation from the organisers

plopped through my letter box offering me a priority, guaranteed place in the 2001 race, as I had been a runner in 2000, I noted the entry fee had risen from £20 to £22. When, a week or two later, a letter appeared in the press asking why the entry fee had risen again – I was not aware it had risen for the 2000 race of course – my concern rose. I began to ask a question or two about costs and discovered, not entirely to my surprise because the media exposure is huge, that the City of Newcastle wrote off its costs to provide all the facilities at the start. This is a fair undertaking because you can imagine the mess left behind by 50,000 runners and probably another 10,000 spectators. It all has to get cleared up. There are other costs the Council carries too; I won't bore you by describing the detail. I was starting to feel uncomfortable. I can do multiplication. £20 times 50,000 runners is one million quid. The whole event is heavily sponsored by BUPA the private healthcare insurers and providers. The best t-shirt of the run incidentally said: 'F**k BUPA-Support the NHS'. Then you have to add in the television coverage, how much was the fee? Just where was all this money going?

I composed a searching letter to the papers. Before dispatching it however, I thought it probably best to check it out with the Leader of the Council and the Chief Executive. They were up the stairs and in my office before you could say Nova International. (Nova is the company who organise the race on behalf of the company that own the name Great North Run.) Did I realise how important the Company was to sport in the region? Did I want to cause an incident and piss these people off? Oh dear, I was back in the real world of opportunity, advantage and intrigue. Nothing is quite what it seems and the spin and gloss of the media can disguise all manner of inequities and exploitation.

So I was persuaded to write at first to the company itself, to ask for their comments. The response was immediate. A very senior executive replied, demanding a meeting with the Chief Executive, the Leader and myself. We met. Amazingly he was completely unaware of the amount of resources he was receiving free from the

Council. I asked him fairly straight on where the money went to and, well, to cut a long story of fencing and imprecision short he confessed to making a six-figure profit that year. He also referred me to the published accounts of the companies involved. I didn't bother, but you could; www.companieshouse.gov.uk is the internet address and the company registration numbers are: Great North Run Ltd 01900256, Nova International 03300783. In fairness the one element I had not taken into consideration was the huge appearance money demanded by not just the top four or five runners but by 20 or 30 of them. Still not a bad profit though!

So two things to remember if you take part in this wonderful event, and it was, at the time, wonderful. First remember someone is making money out of your efforts for charity; secondly, remember the slogan on that t-shirt. Patrick and I neatly turned under the BUPA advertising logo on our race numbers before pinning them on; it's easy to do and each statement counts!

Cycles, rituals and change

The Pedicab had proved a popular idea but it turned out to be a bugger to get hold of an actual vehicle. I had ordered one from the company in Manchester who had brought the model up for the press launch of the idea. Unfortunately they failed to deliver and by June 2000 I had to give up on them. Probably because of all the publicity I had received, a phone call from an acquaintance told me of a Pedicab for sale in Tynemouth. This had a lovely history, having been won in a competition run by an independent radio station. They had asked people to nominate their dream and the winners had their dream come true. Angela, who I bought the Pedicab from, had entered a dream of owning a Pedicab; and she won. Alas her dreams of using it on the promenade from Tynemouth towards Whitley Bay were torpedoed by an unsympathetic North Tyneside Council. I must say I do moan about the lack of progressive thought and action in Newcastle City Council, but compared to many of the others it is a beacon of enlightenment.

So she sold it to me. Or rather to Newcastle Healthy Cities Project who had become partners in the enterprise of setting up a Pedicab service. We had by this time acquired £5,000 from Northern Rock in support of the scheme, courtesy of an old friend, Mike Smith, who I had come to know through a regeneration project in the Elswick ward. Mike had sat on the Board of this project as a representative of the private sector and had demonstrated a true commitment to the difficult task of putting some hope back into an area and a community which had largely collapsed. I was all the more grateful as Mike is a fanatical Sunderland supporter and you will understand from my remarks earlier what stunning generosity this represented.

The earlier instructions to staff of the Council to have nothing to do with the Pedicab had, thankfully, been somewhat relaxed now we had actually obtained one. Indeed some rather more sympathetic souls amongst the officers were being positively helpful. Eventually a training scheme to help people back into employment, which offered a help, advice and city guide service for people in the city centre, called the Newcastle Knights, agreed to ask for volunteers to run a free trip service on the Quayside. A number of 'Knights' did volunteer and on Wednesdays, from June until September, the Pedicab operated along the Quayside giving rides to anyone who wanted one.

June seems to be a busy time in the calendar of the Lord Mayor. A clash of engagements meant that I was unable to take part in the North East celebrations for the opening of the Sustrans National Cycle Network, which took place at the Stadium of Light, ground of Sunderland Football Club. This was a considerable disappointment, however I was able to ensure that the Pedicab itself was present at the event as its fame was now spreading. A couple of days before the event I received an urgent phone call to ask to borrow it. Apparently the publicity people had realised the media opportunity of bringing Hillary Armstrong MP, then the Local Government Minister, who was a principal guest at the opening, into the stadium riding in a Pedicab. So indeed they did and as a result the Pedicab featured on television and in the papers, but without its owner.

I was left in Newcastle unveiling a plaque to Cardinal Basil Hume, the recently deceased Catholic Primate, who was born and brought up in the city. I went to church more during my time acting up and as Lord Mayor than in the previous 35 years put together; and in the next 35 too! I was invited to one single religious event by another religion, a Hindu Festival, and that was it. The Christians are well organised in the networking of the great and the good. Again it is history and tradition. Britain is of course highly unusual in the western world in having an official state religion and that attitude of a relationship between church and state works at local as well as national levels. I find this whole concept of God being on the side of one organised group rather than another completely weird. It is at the height of being oxymoronic in the case of military chaplains. The concept of God being on your troops' side, and not the other lot, seems to be about as directly at odds with the basis of the message of the scriptures as it is possible to be.

I had the opportunity, therefore, to sample several of the different brands of Christianity during my period of office and there is no question the Catholics were head and shoulders ahead in terms of the richness of their rituals. It seems to me that if you want to believe in a deity then you should celebrate that belief in as full a way as possible. The Catholics use poetry and music in a refreshingly broad way to illustrate their celebration of belief. I guess as an old actor it was the sheer theatricality of their services that appealed. Clare, who claims she 'sits on the fence a bit' on God, has a tendency towards the simpler forms of Christianity such as Methodism or even the Quakers; but I cannot escape from the feeling that if you are going to do it then do it in style.

I was very grateful to learn an excellent phrase of definition from a fellow atheist during my year: 'Man created God, not the other way around'. Short, succinct and very much to the point even in its gender politics, I used it on several occasions once I had heard it.

On the evening of the Sustrans and Cardinal Hume events Clare and I attended one of the real highlights of our year; the Daisy Hill Girls Group Millennium Quilt Project. Clare is a textile artist working particularly in silk-screening and for her this was an extra delight, I think, because of the technical variety used. Both of us were just knocked out however by the range of thought and sheer hard work that had gone into producing the images on the 20 or so squares in the quilt. It illustrated some contemporary issues but the over-riding impression I gained was of hope and optimism for the future, which the concept of the Millennium represents at its best.

The girls, their mums and their sisters – there was hardly a man in sight – had come out in force to meet us. Talking with them, first about the quilt but later far more generally about their lives, was a pleasure I came across all too rarely. I have, for most of my life in Newcastle, been directly involved in one community or another, both personally and professionally, and much of the community of the Lord Mayor is not one I would choose to spend time with. These lasses were just so nice it was hard to leave. I even got talking with a few of the mums about politics, well about a political scheme launched by the Council, called Going For Growth.

They wanted information principally, information about what it might mean for their homes. As it happened, I had just received a copy of the glossy brochure the Council had produced to introduce Going For Growth. So I was able to tell them that yes, there were some proposals to demolish houses around about that area. I should explain. In my farewell speech to the Council, on retiring as Lord Mayor, I described Going For Growth as one of the worst community consultation exercise I had ever witnessed in the city. It stands as an example to others of how not to kick off a major exercise in thinking about your town or city. It was a contentious issue, it is less so now although that may not be a good thing, but what is it?

Fifty years ago, Newcastle was still a major old-fashioned northern industrial city at the heart of a major old-fashioned industrial region. It had coal mines, shipyards, heavy engineering, railways and much of the other industry supported those old traditional forms. Coal and the railways had been nationalised, shipbuilding was to follow, it seemed that life was settled and would continue thus forever. A benign socialism encompassed a consensus on the welfare state with neither Labour nor the Conservatives seriously suggesting any alternative. The wider world of capitalism and industry was not, however, standing still. Capitalism is a voracious consumer of people, ideas and resources and as we now can see so clearly, changes and developments elsewhere in the world were undermining the foundations upon which the economy of Newcastle was built. By the 1970s this had begun to turn into a crisis. Coal mining and railways had already suffered significant 'rationalisation'. The famous Dr Beeching had closed many branch lines, and, as Margaret Thatcher was fond of pointing out, the Labour Government of the early 1960's had closed more pits than she did. It has to be said, however, that closing down dozens of tiny inefficient pits is a bit different to closing down an entire indigenous energy industry, which is what she did, but I digress.

The run-down and closure of many of those traditional industries left a huge problem in the residential areas where their workforces lived, virtually all of which had been re-built since the war to varying degrees of quality. Newcastle is a resourceful city, that was my theme, and of course people adapted and changed to the growth of the new industries that came to dominate the economy. Retail, finance, education, health service, local and national government departments and agencies now provide 80 per cent of the region's economy. The people adapted, and moved, leaving those traditional working class residential areas to gradually but inexorably decay.

This decay began to lead to the disintegration of communities in areas, most of which are along the riverside in Newcastle. I have a name for this slow but steady slide into environmental and social disorder: the 'Distillation Effect'. In communities which could support the range of natural abilities, from highly skilled to quite poorly skilled in both the job market and domestic and social areas, the less able were generally sustained by the more able. As work moved away from the riverside communities the more able moved to follow, leaving a higher and higher concentration of the less able behind. As the proportion of less able grew there was no longer the tempering effect of the employed, socially stable, and better paid, and if you like, more sorted out people, to help create a natural balance within the community. This has led, in Newcastle and many other cities with similar declining areas, to the downward spiral most commonly described these days as social exclusion.

So, first the pattern of work changed then gradually the pattern of residential order. The city is therefore faced with two linked but distinct problems. First, districts become run-down, depopulated and dangerous. A part of Elswick, which had suffered this fate, was famously described as 'little Beirut' by the *Guardian* about five years ago. Secondly, our overall population is declining. This depopulation, the haemorrhaging of people from the city, has a slow but very significant effect on those left behind. There are fewer of them to carry the load of supporting the necessary services. Now I am not trying to give a hard luck story here, but we do have a problem in the first place to satisfy the demands placed on the city as a Regional Capital. Social services, economic development and leisure resources all receive a higher demand upon them than you would expect for the numbers in the population. When this is overlaid by a decline in the number of people paying Council and other taxes you can see how their individual contributions are under heavy pressure to rise to meet the demands of needs.

Thus, Going For Growth, which attempts to address both of these problems by tackling them very directly. Embark upon a 15 year programme to reverse the decline in population and, as part of that, take radical action in the declining areas and communities. Part of this strategy utilises industrial land that is either abandoned or nearly so, and turns it into desirable private housing development land. But another part means taking the land on which some of the worst, most declined communities stand; then demolishing their houses and re-building for an entirely new, more up-market, community, replacing largely unemployed working class Council tenants, with largely employed, middle class, owner-occupiers.

Broad sweep social engineering is one way of looking at it.

The generalisation of the decline is quite accurate, it has happened that way, and with it a considerable amount of personal human misery. But the human scale of the broad sweep needed to change also promises disruption and personal distress for many. All the more reason, therefore, to employ all of the Council's knowledge and skills in presentation to those communities most directly affected. Sadly, this was done so poorly that most of those communities came to regard Going For Growth as a classic uncaring, impersonal imposition, by an out of touch autocratic Council.

I have talked about Going for Growth at some length because it really is one of the most important policy development issues the city has faced for many years, perhaps 50, perhaps even 150. You can argue that it parallels the disruption of the old values that burst upon the city as the Industrial Revolution took a strong and widespread grip. It is similarly the result of a fundamental economic shift of wealth generation.

I have also talked about this at some length because it was brought up by women in an affected area during one of the nicest events of our year. And I have talked about it because it raises an old chestnut, a classic dilemma for politicians and others – can the ends justify the means? And if the ends are the inevitable result of progress then surely we have developed a sufficiently sophisticated and humanitarian culture, economy, and society, for the means to be acceptably caring towards those who are caught in the pits we have all created?

I have not talked about the Mansion House much yet. It is the third, or possibly fourth, Mansion House the city has boasted. It is the 'Official Residence' of the Lord Mayor and is used principally for entertainment, presentations, and social events. The building originally consisted of two houses, Thurso House and Kelso House, and was converted to a single dwelling by Sir Arthur Munroe Sutherland, Lord Mayor in 1918-19. He was a fantastically rich merchant and ship-owner who, amongst other acts of philanthropy, built and donated a dental training hospital which is now part of the University of Northumbria at Newcastle, the 'Poly', as it is still affectionately known locally

Sir Arthur lived in the house, which was built in 1876, right up until his death in 1953 when he left it for the use of the Corporation, as it still was called then. It is a magnificent building, of the type that has invariably been bulldozed to make way for luxury flats these days. Indeed it has two such developments as neighbours. It is of no particular historical or architectural interest, in fact I gathered from one architect I entertained there that it is best described as pastiche, architecturally. It is, however, perfect for formal Civic occasions. The building lies within extensive grounds in the suburb of Jesmond, a posh area of the Toon, and must frankly be worth a fortune. Unfortunately the Council do not own it. Sir Arthur's will left the building to the Corporation for use as a Mansion House; however he stipulated that if the Corporation ceased to use it as such then it would revert to his heirs and successors. This was only discovered quite recently when the Leader of a few years ago thought it might be a good scheme to sell off the back garden, itself worth five or six million pounds, and was thwarted when the small print was investigated. There are surviving relatives of Sir Arthur and how they must wish we would decide we no longer need it.

You get to know the house quite well during your year. Its size is intimidating at first but soon Clare and I got feel almost familiar with it. I have already mentioned one or two lunches and dinners held there and in total I guess I probably ate a couple of dozen formal meals there. In fact I will never eat as well again as I did during that year, I ate at most of the major hotel and conference venues in the city, and only one was poor.

But there were many other uses of the Mansion House, in particular charity coffee mornings held regularly on Thursdays. On these occasions, the charity concerned is given access to the house with coffee and scones provided, all for free, and they then invite all their friends and supporters who are expected to make a generous donation. It usually works well and the collection plate never dipped below three figures and, on one occasion, exceeded £600.

We also held receptions for people there. If an international group or conference was in the city then a reception, either at the Civic Centre or the Mansion House, was the order of the day. So it was for the Congress of European Playworkers' Conference, when the Mansion House was the venue. There was nothing particularly special about the event except an out of the blue invitation from the Italian delegation to visit them, in Palermo, Sicily. I thought about as much would come from this as all the other times visitors looked me straight in the eye, told me I must come to visit their city, and then disappeared without trace.

Surprise, surprise – I am on the plane to Rome, and from there to Palermo! It being Sicily, we have endured endless cracks about the Mafia, concrete overcoats, horses' heads, offers we could not refuse, and so on. As it turns out this is actually all very relevant because our host, Leoluca Orlando, has made his name as the anti-Mafia Mayor. In common with most continental Mayors, Leoluca is the senior politician of his Council and is elected for four years at a time. In fact Leoluca is within just over a year of his third and final term as Mayor, three terms being the maximum. Everyone we meet tells us Leoluca is finishing soon and what are they going to do without him? He appears a really genuinely popular figure in the city.

Palermo is an ancient but very run-down city. Sicily as a whole is poor and economically backward, Italy being the approximate reverse of Britain with its wealth and opportunities in the North and poverty in the South. It has, however, been a crossroads in the Mediterranean for several thousand years and the Sicilians claim this gives them the best cuisine in Europe. On the short evidence of our three-day visit I am not going to disagree. We visit cathedrals and theatres which are like cathedrals, doing the tourist round, except that we get into Teatro Massimo which is not yet open to the public again, but will be soon. One evening, after the official business is done we end up, with our new Sicilian friends, taking a walk to the ice-cream parlour. This café is apparently famous throughout the land and the ice cream, this is 2am by the way, is absolutely delicious. We walk back through the back streets towards the city centre and our hotel and come across an undertaker's workshop, with the man going hammer and tongs at coffin building. I expect it is cooler and pleasanter engaging in that kind of manual work at 3am, but the image of the coffin builder hammering away at that time as we saunter through the deserted streets is the abiding memory of the city.

Leoluca himself provides the other memory. He has a long political career and comes from a noble Sicilian family. At one point in the early 1990s, he tells us, the Mafia bosses decreed that three people must die: Falcone, Borsolino, and Orlando. Falcone and Borsolino were blown to smithereens on the road from the airport to the city by a high explosive device planted in the road. Leoluca claims that he was so popular with the 'foot soldiers' that they went to the bosses and said that he must be spared. Spared he obviously was, though they take no chances. When he travels in the city it is in a four or five vehicle convoy, he is accompanied at all times by at least two armed guards. They are so discreet it's a marvel – every so often you remember that the reason they are not engaged in the business around them is because they are armed and watching.

He is something of an international figure, travelling around to promote his message that Sicily is ready for business and that the Mafia are not a romantic secret society, not a career of honour, not an inevitable feature of the Sicilian landscape; but are what they would be called anywhere else in the world, organised criminals.

It's a murky old world, and a confusing one. Leoluca reckoned that a very senior national politician was a Mafia man, but that also he was Leoluca's protector against the hit squads. Then, just to add further intrigue to the situation, a newspaper article in early 2001 reported that Leoluca himself had now been accused of being a Mafia plant and was under investigation.

That, as it turned out, was that for international trips. I was to get at least two more promises of invitations to China but, as with the previous offers, nothing ever came of them. Still I got to Durham City on a couple of occasions and what finer city is there (other than Newcastle, of course)?

The High Sheriff of Durham had invited me to attend 'Matins for the Courts' at Durham Cathedral, which I happily concede knocks spots off Newcastle's cathedrals, and most others in Britain too. This was obviously a regular ritual event, but turned out to have a couple of quirks to it this particular year. Firstly it used to be the form for the High Sheriff to invite all the Civic dignitaries for lunch afterwards but, for reasons that were obscure then and are now completely forgotten, this had not transpired. Frankly I could not have cared less, but when we arrived it was clear from the Mayor of Durham City that a diplomatic incident of major significance was in progress. I was issued with a briefing. This consisted of ensuring that on exit from the service we all turned left towards the room we had changed in, rather than right to join the main party of dignitaries for a photo-call. It was what is known as an official snub. Honestly, the way people behave; you didn't invite me for tea so I'm not going to play with you, ya boo.

The second quirk was even more fascinating. About 20 years ago a Tyneside surgeon named Paul Vickers was sent to jail for murdering his wife, allegedly by poisoning her through medication (she had a long term debilitating disease). He always maintained his innocence but several attempts at appeal failed. He is now freed having served his sentence. So here we were in Durham Cathedral at a service for the good works and offices for the entire judicial system from Teesside to Berwick upon Tweed attended by a Lord of Appeal, High Court Judges, Chief Constables, and many other legal dignitaries; and the sermon was astonishing.

It was delivered by The Reverend Canon Eric James, and except for a few general remarks at the beginning and end, the entire sermon was dedicated to a plea for a pardon for Paul Vickers, and, implicitly, a slagging off of the criminal justice system. The case has, as I have outlined, been round the judicial system pretty thoroughly with no positive outcome for Mr Vickers. That of course is not to make any judgement on his innocence, plenty of innocents have been banged up, that's for sure. The Reverend Canon, it transpired, had been at Oxford University with Paul Vickers and his sermon was pretty short on legal inconsistency and procedures, and pretty long on the fact he knew him from Oxford. In fact it seemed to me that the main thrust of his argument was that a Balliol man would never knock off his missus.

As we were snubbing the main dignitaries party I never did get to gauge the reaction of the Lord of Appeal and so on who were present, but it did remind me that just beneath the surface lies a powerful old boys network. Though not, I guess, powerful enough to have kept Paul Vickers out of jail in the first place. The Reverend Canon obviously felt strongly enough to use the occasion for his plea and I hope he felt it worthwhile; I think we can be pretty confident he won't get a return booking.

Talking of matters legal, it was around this time that I acquired the dubious honour of being the first Lord Mayor in living memory to have his wallet nicked whilst on duty. That's in addition to the one I mentioned earlier, pinched from my house. It was not a good year for wallets but it was a good year for firsts. I think I was almost certainly the first Lord Mayor to abseil off the tower of the Civic Centre and all credit to my successor who did it too. I hope we have set up a tradition! With the Pedicab and the Great North Run that was a trio of firsts.

Football and freedom

Of course much of the life of the Lord Mayor is about firsts. You hold the office for one short year. It is an extraordinary period of time where your opportunities to do and see things, and to meet and talk to people of fame, power and influence is unparalleled. Looking back, now, from a distance of a few months, there is a slight temptation to think, 'if only I could do it again I would do X, Y or Z so much better'. No doubt that may be true, but the essence of the office is that it is only one very intensive year. Actually there were a few of the dull and the interminable engagements, although they fade much quicker from memory than the fun and interesting ones.

Most of us lead fairly predictable and routine lives, I guess, and this year was special for the elements of change and variety on a daily basis. We met from time to time, people of especial courage, ability and determination. One such group of people was all those involved in the ASDA Millennium Great North Transplant Games, to give it its full title. I did not even know that such a thing as the Transplant Games existed, but in late July they were held on Tyneside, principally in Gateshead whose athletics support is internationally known, but also in Newcastle and South Tyneside. As you might imagine, the one entry criterion is to have received a transplant. The games were initially started by Dr Ross Taylor, a now retired surgeon, as an innovative way of encouraging physical exercise through sport for transplant patients.

Making the body work physically is considered to divert its

thoughts away, as it were, from rejecting the transplant received. Patients had often become very run down in the period leading up to the transplant and needed to get fit again. There are a whole host of reasons behind the Games that seem as obvious to me as the therapeutic effect of art making for users of the Arts Studio I described earlier. Initially they all had to struggle hard to get support for the event but it has grown over the years and now encompasses quite a significant community. Naturally the community has also grown as transplants have become more successful and more frequent, but the word community is, for once, used in a very real sense. It was what was so outstanding about the event. People come from all over the country to meet up year after year. They usually know each other, or if they don't they soon get to during the four or five days. The sense of a group of people caring for and supporting one another was incredibly strong. It pervaded the atmosphere at every event we went to and is obviously a great tribute to those surgeons and other medical professionals who have nurtured and supported the movement from its inception. Not that they in any way control or dominate the event. On the contrary it is very obvious that transplant patients themselves control events and proceedings with the medical people acting in their support not as their directors.

It is a community that really does know the meaning of life. Its members either would not have life, or would have it in significantly reduced quality, were it not for their transplants. Three powerful emotional memories stand out from those four days the Games were in town. First, the end of the farewell dinner where around 1,300 people stood, held hands, and sang *You'll Never Walk Alone*. Secondly, the final of the 200 metres where two competitors ran neck and neck well ahead of the pack until, about 50 yards out, one of them tripped. The other, without even thinking about it, stopped to pick him up and make sure he was all right. The third was a simple display board in the refreshment area that displayed messages from the family and friends of donors, remembering their lost loved ones, but in addition celebrating the renewed life they had been able to offer others.

I met Bobby Robson, manager of Newcastle United, on several occasions during the year. The first was not when I took part in a tour of the club's newly re-furbished stadium a couple of weeks before the 2000-2001 season kicked off. That was a slightly touchy occasion as I recall. The ground improvements were fine, wonderful in fact, and St James' Park is one of the best-equipped and provided stadia in the country. No, the trouble arose from the appalling public relations of the club who had decided, with no consultation, that it was necessary to shift about 2,000 supporters out of their, in many cases, very long established seats. Well that is not strictly true, they were offered an opportunity to stay. The problem was that the plans for the refurbishment of the ground entailed a vast increase in corporate hospitality and the accompanying seats. So yes they could stay, but the cost of the seat rose by around 400 per cent. This had, towards the end of the previous season, provoked bitter controversy and acrimony. Indeed, I had myself stood throughout an entire game as a protest against the Board's high handed actions; and joined in the chants of abuse. Six fans had actually gone as far as taking out a High Court action against the club which, of course, they subsequently lost.

So there was I, in the company of the Chairman and a number of top club executives, not to mention the Council's Chief Executive and a number of senior Councillors, inspecting the newly created facilities. Well everything was fine until the end when we arrived at a hospitality suite which was actually finished and started to tuck in to a spot of buffet lunch. After a few minutes the Chairman banged his glass and proceeded to make a short speech about how wonderful everything was and how wonderful the Council was in helping them achieve their development. This was not on the order of business I had been provided with and when, as he finished, he made it obvious I was expected to respond I was struck by an acute moral dilemma. After all I had been singing rude songs about the

man and his executives barely weeks before. I did not endear myself by telling the assembled company that in my view the Club was on trial with the fans for the forthcoming season. This went down, as they say, like a cup of cold vomit. Towards the end of my remarks, struggling desperately to find a half decent compromise remark to finish, I suddenly struck on the one point of agreement we all had – that the team should be successful out on the park in the coming ten months. This brought what felt like a very relieved 'hear hear' from the assembled company.

Subsequently the Chairman and I developed a pantomime routine which no doubt hid our mutual suspicions of one another. Whenever he met me he would bow deeply and say 'My Lord Mayor'. To which I would respond in like manner with, 'My Chairman'. Tradition of course means that the Chairman offers the Lord Mayor two of the best seats in the house for the entire season so we kept running into one another, although conversation did not flow. One thing you can say about the Chairman is that French is not his strongpoint. One Saturday afternoon in mid season I entered the lift to go up two floors to the level of my seat. At the first level up the lift stopped, the doors opened, and in came the

Chairman grasping a bulky briefcase. Quite why he was walking round his own football club at 2.30 on a Saturday afternoon of a match carrying a big briefcase was a mystery never solved. However, earlier that week he had sold a French player, Alain Goma, for a few million quid. So, quick as a flash, after we had done the bowing routine, I asked if the briefcase contained the money from selling Alain. 'No', replied the Chairman, 'it's the money from Goma'. Well maybe it was my lousy French accent.

I met Bobby Robson for the first time at the re-branding of the 'Gossy', Gosforth Park Hotel a posh hotel on the northern outskirts of the city. I think the chain of hotels it belonged to had been taken over by another chain of hotels, so they wanted to make a splash. They certainly made a meal of the afternoon. Bobby was flown in by helicopter from the Club's training ground, near Durham; half a funfair was set up; there were sideshows, prizes and the obligatory buffet meal. It is remarkable how much money business will spend on parties, launches and the like.

Bobby is quite as shrewd as his reputation makes out. I guess he has spent a fair bit of time with late teenage boys over the years but when we met in the interval of the Royal Shakespeare Company production of *Henry V* at the Theatre Royal, a couple of months later, he took one look at my son as I introduced him and guessed his age (17 years and nine months) exactly. Bobby was quite intrigued by the Shakespeare and I tried to explain the basic plot was nationalist xenophobia – nasty, devious, slimy frogs versus bold upstanding English patriots who get all the good speeches. He listened politely but I think he was most interested in the stamina needed and displayed by the actor playing Henry. Well that's his life I suppose, physical fitness combined with special skills.

It certainly is great to have the Theatre Royal in the city, and the annual RSC season which is now 25 years old. The old Tyne and Wear Council helped us take over the building in the early 1970s when its commercial owners were seriously considering turning it into a Bingo Hall. Remember Bingo was really big in those days. Now it's run by a Trust half comprised of Councillors and half of outsiders, mostly business or ex business men. It stands near the top of Grey Street, which has been described as the most beautiful street in England. Certainly the imposing ionic pillared portico of the theatre and the sweep of the street as it descends the bank of the Tyne in a gentle curve is a very fine sight indeed. I am sorry about all this blatant promotion of the city as a tourist destination but if you haven't visited us or seen Grey Street then you should.

It was not a particularly good year for Bobby on the pitch with unfortunate injuries and one or two new players not quite coming up to expectations. It has been a frustrating time for the fans over the past few years since Kevin Keegan left. Two rather fortuitous FA Cup runs have taken us to Wembley where we totally outclassed on both occasions and a slightly unlucky semi final defeat the following year are all we have managed. Gone, for the moment, are the days when a game against Manchester United was a potential Premier League championship decider. Interestingly the departure of Keegan and the subsequent decline in performances on the pitch coincides with the flotation of the Club on the Stock Market. Both the Chairman and his predecessor, whose family still own a large slice, became the very rich men they are during the ideology of licenced greed encouraged by Thatcher's Conservative government. I am yet to be convinced as to just where their values lie.

I think my feelings towards the people who own and control the Club are best summed up by the story of the Cowgate Kestrels. Cowgate is in the north-west of the city not far from the centre and certainly within sight of St James' Park. Actually, just about everything within 20 miles is within sight of the new stadium as it now dominates the city's skyline, but that's a story of business, tradition and planning permission for another time. Cowgate is close to the hallowed ground and in Cowgate, 20 odd years ago, a women's' football team was started. Just a fun kickabout thing for lasses initially, as women's football was very underdeveloped at the time. By the late 80s and early 90s, when I first came across them, they had begun to develop into a seriously good team who were climbing up through the newly formed leagues. They were desperate to become attached to Newcastle United, to become their women's team. As I had an opportunity to meet the then Chairman through Council business I put to him this possibility. I was rewarded with a phone call from the Chief Executive to whom I put the case and gave the contact names. Alas, nothing came of it. The reason I was first involved was through a Council officer, Jane Ashworth, who worked in a job dedicated to the Elswick Ward. In her spare time, however, one of her great interests was the Kestrels. She then moved jobs and I drifted out of touch with both her and the Kestrels. In the spring of 2001, towards the end of my year, Jane rang up. 'I have written a book about the Kestrels, would you officiate at the launch.' I was of course delighted.

Jane's book rejoices in the title of *Kicking the Boys' Balls* and is an interesting read (ISBN: 1872204759). I was keen to catch up with the team's fortunes. In the intervening eight years or so the Kestrels had continued to make progress through the leagues. Spurned by Newcastle United again in the mid 90s they had joined forces with Blyth Spartans, one of the most famous non-league clubs in the North East, and become the Blyth Spartan Kestrels. In this guise they had won promotion in May 2000 to the national first division, the Premier League of women's football. Still in touch with their origins, and just as keen to become the Newcastle United team, they approached the club once again. Surely you would think that after making such progress, after the national and media profile of women's football had developed so much, after all the Club's rhetoric about being an integral part of the Geordie community, surely this time they would agree?

At first things appeared to go well. The Club's new Chief Executive was keen on the phone and seemed to suggest that they would be extremely interested. After two days however he called back with a flat no. No discussion and just an apology. In my view there is only one place that instruction could have come from, the Chairman's office. So now we compound short sightedness with tragedy. After the rejection there was only one place for the Kestrels to go. Within a week they were the official Sunderland women's football team and you can follow their progress in the national newspapers each season (if they stay up of course) under that name which any true Toon supporter can barely utter. What a waste!

Actually I am going to be honest and say something only an incomer could find easy. From the point of view of service and caring for the ordinary fan, Sunderland is the superior club. I will still cheer as loudly as the next fan when Sunderland lose, and get depressed for a week if they beat us at St James' Park like they have the past two seasons (not this year, they were lucky to escape with a draw). We couldn't believe last season. Alan Shearer of all people missing the penalty to bring us level deep in the second half, god it still sends a shiver of depression down my back. But if I were asked by an uncommitted football fan moving to the area I would have to tell them that Newcastle did not offer the best deal. This will not endear me to Niall and Biffa at www.nufc.com who run a wonderful unofficial website, so in order to ingratiate myself with them can I just say that if you want to find out all the latest about the Toon, they run the best site by a country mile.

I shouldn't be too hard on Alan Shearer who would have been as gutted as the rest of us that evening he missed the penalty. Alan has had a magnificent career, hopefully, as I write in the summer of 2001, not yet over. In March he was one of five people to whom I awarded the Freedom of the City on behalf of the Council. The others were Nick Brown MP, who was a Councillor in the city before rising to the Cabinet (he got sacked soon after the award but I would bet on him being back); Lord Glenamarra, who as Ted Short was first a City Councillor, then an MP, and finally Deputy Prime Minister; Sage Software plc, who I have already talked about; and Jonathon Edwards.

Sadly Jonathon was hop, skip and jumping somewhere on the

day of the ceremony and could not be with us, but all the others turned up and a quite excellent party it was.

Nick Brown was just one month in to what I suspect was the worst time of his political life, the Foot and Mouth crisis, and interestingly had brought with him both the President of the National Farmers Union and his Liberal Democrat shadow minister Lembit Opik (he comes from a Latvian family). Lembit was also a Newcastle City Councillor before being elected to Parliament and is a nice guy so it was great to see him again. How interesting too, seeing how well the three of them got on over the crisis.

Lord Glenamarra is Chancellor of the University of Northumbria, and I had attended a half-day of their degree awards some months before. Despite being in his late eighties he had stood to present over 200 degree certificates to students that afternoon and I was even more impressed when I found out that he did it for three days. That's six award sessions on the trot. At a dinner I was invited to after the awards had all been presented, he told a wonderful story of a meeting he had, I think when he was Leader of the Council, with T. Dan Smith. The Poly and the Civic Centre were being planned at the time and the two of them sat down and worked out where the new buildings were going to go and which streets of houses would have to make way for them. Once decided T. Dan looked at him and said, 'Right Ted, you better go and tell the people.' As this story was being told at the exact time that our Going for Growth strategy was getting panned right left and centre I think the story had a certain relevance.

Alan Shearer, of course, ensured a packed Banqueting Hall for the ceremony and much TV coverage. I believe even my Mum and Dad saw me on the national news. He brought his wife and two older children who all signed my Lord Mayor's guestbook, so I must be one of very few people to have the autographs of four Shearers.

I cannot let the sporting year go without its triumph. I grew up more as a soccer than a rugger fan but I enjoy most sports. Since my son took up playing, I have understood the modern rules of Rugby Union a little better and I even went to watch the Newcastle Falcons twice during their championship-winning season a few years ago. They dipped slightly after that but in the 2000/2001 season they got good again. They fought their way to the cup final, sponsored by some awful brand of bland carbonated beer. So down to Twickers it was to watch them. They took an early lead but then lost it and gradually fell behind. Midway through the second half our prospects looked bleak. Then we scored, then again. Time ticked on and we were into the last minute. A lineout right on the opposition's line goes unexpectedly in our favour. The ball flies across the field in front of their line and suddenly we have two, no three, spare men and over they go for the match-winning try. Fantastic, just what you hope a cup final will be like. The Falcons have really invested in a youth development policy and the dividends are beginning to pay off. I expect them to be a major force in English rugby for some time to come. It was a real pleasure, a couple of months later, to host a reception for the team and the club to congratulate them on bringing a solid piece of silverware back to the city.

Bridging the gap

The launch of *Kicking the Boys' Balls* was by no means the only book launch I officiated at during my year, far from it. Over the past ten years, Newcastle Libraries have been slowly but steadily developing a publishing arm. You should see its name, Tyne Bridge Publishing, on the cover of this book if everything has gone according to plan. From simple stapled early publications, largely of archive photographs of areas of the city – *Bygone Elswick, Gone but not Forgotten,* etc – they have gradually developed a wider and wider range of books and subjects. Now their books are commercially printed with proper glossy covers and with a catalogue of over 80 titles, and having recently published their first novel, they are now an established and respected small publisher. I have always believed in the potential of public services to deliver marketplace solutions and initiatives at least as competently as the private sector so I was always ready to support their enterprises. I launched four publications for them during the year, all different and all interesting. In fact it was at the launch of *Swan Hunter: the Pride and the Tears* that I first tentatively ventured to the staff of Tyne Bridge Publishing that I had considered what fun it would be to write about my year. They were wonderfully supportive and encouraging. It's for you, of course, to decide whether their enthusiasm was justified!

In the autumn of 2000, in a shipbuilding yard on the north bank of the Tyne in Wallsend, just beyond the boundary of Newcastle, one of the new wonders of Tyneside began to take shape. The

Gateshead Millennium Bridge is popularly known as the 'blinking eye' bridge and is the first ever pedestrian bridge over the Tyne. Actually I am pleased to say that it has both pedestrian and cycle lanes, which is another welcome boost for cycling in the area. Strictly speaking, of course, this particular event should not be part of this chronicle as the bridge is 100 per cent Gateshead's idea and initiative. However 2000 also brought a new partnership and understanding between the Borough of Gateshead and the City of Newcastle. A partnership based on the recognition that in the new century our long-term rivalry was a handicap in sustaining our economy and our communities. A partnership we hope will culminate in becoming the European City of Culture in 2008.

The bridge links the Newcastle's Quayside, newly re-built and regenerated by the Tyne and Wear Development Corporation, with the new revitalised Gateshead Quays where two massive new cultural developments are being constructed. The 'blinking eye' is actually mis-named; it does not blink at all, it tilts. Nevertheless it is a very special bridge, unique in fact, as no other bridge moves in such a way. The reason for the tilt is of course to allow moderate sized ships and boats to pass through and beyond it, upstream. I am told that, technically, the clearance of the tilted bridge is the same as the clearance of the road deck of the Tyne Bridge so it should make no difference to river traffic. Except that, as always, it is not that simple. For years the Royal Navy has brought boats up to Newcastle Quayside to moor just downstream of the Tyne Bridge; but now the new bridge is a couple of hundred metres further downstream and they cannot reach their traditional berth. I believe the military reason is that in the event of war and a ship being upstream from the now installed 'blinking eye', it could be trapped there if the tilting mechanism were sabotaged. All sounds a little bit far fetched to me but that was the quoted reason. Now a new berth for the Navy has to be dredged out a little further downstream.

The bridge is absolutely lovely. A shining steel arc that promotes all that is best on Tyneside. Designed and built in the region, just like the 'Angel of the North' incidentally, it is a proud example of the skills the workforce of the North East still possess, and their ability to adapt and innovate. The only slight blot on the landscape is Gary's piles! Gary is the Harbourmaster for the Port of Tyne and at his insistence the bridge is protected by huge 'crash barriers' on either side, supported on large and intrusive piles. They impose on the graceful aesthetics of its curves something rotten. Someone should start a campaign for the 'Relief of Gary's Piles'!

So, the bridge was finished and ready in the yard to be transported upstream to its site. The second largest floating crane in the world was engaged to move it. *Asian Hercules II* is enormous. When, after hanging around the Tyne for nearly a month waiting for the right weather conditions, she finally lifted the bridge and proceeded upstream it looked like a toy hanging from her huge jib. Indeed the bridge continued to look like a toy for the whole week *Asian Hercules II* remained in position on the Quayside. It was only after the giant crane retreated downstream that the bridge itself could be appreciated. If you have not seen this latest addition to the famous bridges across the Tyne gorge then you should. If you have not seen any of the bridges, well all I can say is your life is incomplete.

What is remarkable in fact about the Tyneside of the 21st century is just how different it is from expectations. If I had a pound for every person I met during the year who was so surprised at what they found they felt the need to remark upon it, well I would not be a rich man, but you take the point.

The partnership with Gateshead really is a project to defy history. I talked before about the fact that the Corporation of Newcastle once annexed Gateshead in the middle of the 16th century and that kind of set the tone for succeeding years. The Provost of St Nicholas's Cathedral told me of a conversation he had with a volunteer driver at one of the big hospitals in Newcastle. New to the area the Provost knew little of the history of antagonism between the two sides of the river. Chatting away, as one does in these situations, he remarked that he must travel all over collecting and returning patients. On being told that sometimes he went as far as Ashington (about 30 miles north) the Provost asked if he got as far as Durham to the south. 'Oh no', the volunteer replied, 'they sent me to Gateshead once, but I asked them not to do it again.'

So you can see what a tradition of attitudes the partnership has to overcome. Yet only if we can re-visit and re-interpret our old traditions, habits and attitudes can we make progress.A Field Marshall was the last person I expected to give me confirmation that this approach was what was needed, but it was precisely from that source that such advice was offered. Tradition that stands still ossifies and dies was the advice of Field Marshall the Lord Inge at a dinner which we both attended. Traditions have to be living, growing, and developing to remain strong. It is advice the Freemen of Newcastle should heed.

I have already talked about the Freemen, their close and very long historical link with the Corporation and then City Council as it evolved, and the one thing that does keep them beyond an archaic historical pantomime – the Town Moor. If you are not familiar with the Town Moor then briefly it is 388 hectares of land to the immediate north of the city centre. It is nearly all grassland, and trees are mostly confined to lining the verges of the roads on its borders

It was time for the Michaelmas Gild, one of their three times a year symbolic meetings where the Lord Mayor presides. At these events the Chairman of the Stewards of the Freemen reports to the Lord Mayor on their recent activities, problems they encounter which they would like help with, and any other issues relevant to the relationship between the City and the Freemen. The Lord Mayor replies, usually in a simple formal manner, and then a senior legal officer of the city lists the issues between the two parties, as the Council perceives them. Last year as stand-in I had mostly just lapped up the magnificent surroundings and enjoyed the panto. This year I decided to be a little pushy.

Well actually I was downright naughty. I had tacitly agreed with the Leader of Council, in a slightly tense negotiation before he would recommend me to the Labour Group as Lord Mayor, to abide by a set of protocols of behaviour. This included taking advice from him or his deputy, or from the chief Executive, on 'politically sensitive issues'. Now there were not any 'politically sensitive issues' about the Town Moor going on at the time, but unfortunately I was about to create one. To make it worse, I made sure people knew about it by sending out a Press Release without consulting either the Leader or the Chief Executive. Well they would only have said no, and I was only going to get one opportunity to make this statement in a such way that notice might be taken of it. And actually I had already defied the Protocol with public comments about how dire the Going for Growth process was, and nobody had bothered me

What I said in the Press Release was:

LORD MAYOR SLAMS TOWN MOOR MANAGEMENT 'BORING AND UNIMAGINATIVE'

In his address to the Michaelmas Gild of the Freeman of the City, the Lord Mayor, Cllr Peter Thomson, criticised the boring and unimaginative use of the Town Moor. He called for a new initiative to use 'this most wonderful resource past generations have left for us' in tune with modern environmental needs.

'It is 35 years since a bold and imaginative plan for bio-diversification on the Town Moor was proposed and over ten since the matter was last considered. It really is unacceptable that a resource like the Moor, which most cities would give their eye teeth for, is so blatantly underused and taken for granted', claimed Cllr Thomson.

'It seems to me,' he continued, 'that all the Freemen are really interested in is the hereditary right exercised by a handful of their number to graze their cattle, and the money they make during the Hoppings

'We should be able to make much more than that of this birthright, because it does not 'belong' to the Freeman, it belongs to the city and its people.

'Section 8(1) Town Moor Act 1988 says the Moor is an 'area of open space [maintained] in the interests of the inhabitants of the city, so that it shall continue to both satisfy herbage right and to afford air and exercise for the enjoyment of the public'.

'We do much in the city to encourage environmental diversity including wildlife corridors, interpretation, and planting schemes. Why is there no coherent scheme for the Town Moor?

'New plantations to form copses with a more enclosed and intimate landscape where woodland habitats can develop.

'Develop wetland habitats along the natural line of the Sandyford Burn and in one or two other areas.

'Improve the floristic and invertebrate diversity of the grasslands.

'Promotion and interpretation through published guides, other promotional printed and electronic literature, and 'face to face' activities.

'Celebrate the Town Moor as a resource for residents, visitors, tourists and investors.

'These are just some of the considerations which should be explored.

'I hope before the next Gild we can see some knocking of heads together to make some progress on these issues. Future generations will have reason to be grateful to those who understand a vision for the future, today.'

The press did actually use the 'boring and unimaginative' quote in one report but by and large their comments focussed on the issues. At the Gild itself I used a lot of the phrases from the Press Release – as usual I had written no notes for my speech so I had to rely on it – but I wrapped it around with the usual polite diplomatic language. Afterwards one or two of them took it upon themselves to remind of their ancient rights, over the buffet lunch. One venerable old buffer told me a story I actually knew. In the early 19th century, I believe it was, a group of speculative coal miners set up on the Moor and began excavating. The Freemen, armed with cudgels and the like, forcibly evicted them.

If I had not sent out the Press Release probably nothing much more would have happened. However, when the Chairman of the Stewards' Committee, the body which runs the Freemen, returned to his desk after lunch I think he had one or two press enquiries.

At about 2.30 that afternoon, snoozing quietly at my desk in the Lord Mayor's Chambers, I was awakened by the news that the Leader and Chief Executive were on their way to see me. We had what I believe can be described as a 'robust' conversation. Actually they were kind of smiling, but we both knew I was pushing it. I had to exercise careful judgement here. The Lord Mayor really should be above day to day politics, that is only right, and to deliberately court publicity using the Office could easily become counter productive. The Office is ancient and well respected and I would not want to bring it into disrepute, or to find myself marginalised within it. I still had seven months to go at that point. I knew I could do more for the city, and my own ideas, by retaining a degree of trust within the Council. On the other hand, I did have a perfectly good point.

This story has a bit of a happy ending too. Discussiuons progressed between the Freemen and the Council's environmental officers and I believe real progress is being made in improving both the diversity of the grasslands and the public interpretation. Best of all, the Freemen have agreed to allow me to plant a small copse on the Moor. In fact I am joining forces with Pitch and Mary Wilson, the Mayor and Mayoress of Gateshead while we held office in Newcastle, in this scheme. Pitch and Mary, alongside the other Tyne and Wear Mayors and Mayoresses, became great friends during the year and they have a great regard for nature and the environment. With help and support from Viscount Ridley we will plant trees from both his and Pitch and Mary's nurseries to commemorate the millennium, our wonderful year, and the new spirit of partnership between Newcastle and Gateshead.

21 Reasons for being Lord Mayor

One reason for keeping on the right side of the powers that be was to protect a project which Clare and I had planned. The 21 Debates, part of Agenda 21, were intended to stimulate public discussion and interest in wider political issues. We planned to hold eight.

Agenda 21 arose from the Rio Earth Summit of 1992 where an agenda for the 21st century was debated and conceived. Attended by Heads of Government from most of the world's nations, the Summit took a long hard look at where the planet was heading. Broadly speaking, its conclusions were that subsidiarity is the way forward. As I pointed out in my inaugural speech, a simple interpretation of that much misunderstood word is 'trust the people'. Impossible, of course, for politicians to implement seriously, but wonderful to boost the rhetoric level.

Clare and I, naively perhaps, took the principles and concepts of Rio seriously. We felt very deeply that the conclusions reached were fundamental to civilised survival of the planet and its peoples, and we determined to do what we could to keep the spirit of this debate in the public eye. One of the principles of subsidiarity is to do what you can where you can and we had an opportunity to do a little through our brief tenure of prominent public office.

In the ten years since the Summit, it seemed to Clare and me that two things had happened. First, the concept of Agenda 21 had entered the general consciousness as being solely concerned with the environment. Secondly, after an initial rush of enthusiasm, it

was being quietly forgotten. We wanted to counter both the misconception and the marginalisation.

I suppose in a sense the issues are about the environment, but only in the sense that the environment *is* the whole planet. For those world leaders in Rio ten years ago, the outcomes were cast in terms of the future of the planet. Its future is about politics and how people are part of the political processes, or not part of them. It is about economics and finite material resources. It is about the way we govern, control and organise ourselves at all levels: community, city, region, nation, and globally.

To try and tease out as many of the issues as possible we spent some time looking for a down to earth way of describing what is a intricate and complex inter-relationship. It was not easy, though we did quickly find a marvellous Albert Einstein quote: 'Whenever we tug one strand of the universe we quickly find it is attached to everything else.' We spent some time agreeing a set of principles which defined what we felt Agenda 21 should be about, and I include our definitions in an appendix.

It was quite a list and quite a lot of ideas and concepts. We had some help with it all from the Sustainable Cities Research Institute of Northumbria University. Sustainability is one of the great current buzzwords and buzz concepts, but it is also sensible and practical. They were helpful in defining the philosophy behind the debates and agreed to become joint sponsor with Clare and myself. Four debates would be held in a city centre venue and four in the Cluny Warehouse in the Ouseburn Valley.

The city centre debates would feature two 'protagonists' arguing in traditional debate form for and against a proposition. For these we decided upon: 'Quangos or Local Democracy: which delivers for the people?'; 'School Governance'; 'Elected Mayors'; and 'Regional Government: Vital step for democracy or unnecessary bureaucracy?'

The Cluny debates would have a panel of four or five 'experts' who would answer audience questions 'Question Time' style on a broad topic. After some agonising these broad topics were agreed as: 'Finance and Debt'; 'Environment, Waste, Recycling and the City's Ecology'; 'Health'; and 'Arts and Culture'.

There would be one of each type of debate each month and we kicked off in February 2001. Although the poorest attended of the Cluny debates, 'Finance and Debt' was in many ways one of the most fascinating. We had two panellists from a 'traditional' banking background, an old friend Dr Fred Robinson (a well-known radical socialist academic), a speaker for Credit Unions, and a theologist with a special interest in social justice. It was fascinating because of areas of agreement. A question was asked about a guaranteed social wage for everyone, a radical idea I haven't heard mentioned since the 70s, and lo and behold there was widespread support for it across the panel members.

Giving everyone a guaranteed social wage abolishes the benefits and unemployment system at a stroke whilst creating a pool of labour to be distributed where it is most needed by the state. This was an idea which, when I heard it in the 70s, was tainted by being the basis of the employment policies of the eastern block countries – Johnny Russian's evil empire. Today, ironically, there are many millions from the old Soviet block who would give their eye-teeth to go back to that particular aspect of life in the old regime. Markets brought them pop music and jeans; it also brought poverty wages and unemployment.

Inevitably globalisation emerged as an issue in the debate, as it clearly has a major effect on debt and financial markets. The theme was to be repeated in one form or another at nearly every one of the 21 Debates series. You cannot escape from it today.

Globalisation lies right at the core of Agenda 21. Some people don't like the direction of globalisation, witness the extent of escalating violence and demonstrations at world economic conference events, but it is a fact of contemporary life. It's here whether we like it or not and the questions are all about how we can deal with and control it, not whether we want it or not.

In a world where information has become the most valuable commodity and where that information can be transmitted around the entire planet in a matter of microseconds we must recognise that we can only retain control by addressing the issues on a global scale.

The debate underlined the concept that the poor pay the highest price for the monetary system, both locally and globally. Local Credit Unions make an important difference. There are other financial measures which keep a local economy local by circulating money within the region. These include revolving loans and other schemes to invest in housing and business development avoiding the City of London system. Such schemes do exist in the region, but always as minor measures. It would need a more comprehensive effort to make a real difference.

In December 2000 we approached both the editor of the *Journal* regional daily, and the head of the regional BBC to ask for their support for the Debates. Both responded most positively and this genuinely heartened me. Both agreed to be co-sponsors and to support and publicise the Debates as they occurred.

The BBC agreed to sponsor Mike Parr, presenter of Radio Newcastle's topical debate and phone in programme, *The Zoo*, to be the chair of the four Any Questions panels, and they recorded and broadcast the first debate. I have appeared as a guest on *Mike Parr's Morning Zoo* on a number of occasions, and found him astute and probing. He was an excellent chair for those four debates, contributing much to keep a lively flow of argument going. What really works in those situations is pinning the panellists down into disagreeing or contradicting each other. Then the sparks begin to fly and it all gets interesting. Mike trod the fine line between catalysing argument, and alienating the participants, with skill.

The editor of the *Journal* published an article on the whole series by their Political Correspondent and then an article on the morning of each debate outlining the particular issues under discussion.

The first of the formal debates was on Quangos – QUasi-Autonomous Non Governmental OrganisationS. I had originally lined up two speakers locally famous for not getting on. The first, Alistair Balls, had run the Tyne and Wear Development Corporation from 1987 to 1997 and was now the chief executive of the Centre For Life. The other was the Councillor who had so vigorously tried to stop the Centre happening. It would have been a great spat but unfortunately the Councillor involved, having agreed in the December to take on Alistair, withdrew in late January.

At short notice the Leader of the Council very kindly stood in. My idea for this debate came from seeing the development of Newcastle's Quayside by the Development Corporation who were unelected and largely unaccountable. But would such a comprehensive development have ever gone ahead with the Council in charge? I think not, and that was my theme. In the event Alistair and Tony agreed with each other far too much for a good argument. Although what they said – that the selected business skills of people in Quangos working in partnership with the democratically accountable institutions was a powerful combination – makes good sense to me.

For the issue of school governance I was interested in talking about Local Management of Schools. This is the process introduced by the Conservatives in the mid 90s, and enthusiastically carried forward by the Labour government, to cut out the local Education Authority from any meaningful responsibility for actually running schools. Instead the responsibilities (and money) are given direct to the school governors. Governors are voluntary and very much part time. They are simply not equipped and skilled at the professional tasks of running a school. So the Head Teacher becomes, in effect, the chief executive of the business which is the school. The Head Teacher is main professional advisor to the Governors whose principal concern is to keep their business afloat.

This is not so bad in a secondary school, most of which are the equivelant of a moderate sized business, turning over a couple of million a year. However Primary schools are different, much smaller businesses, and it's becoming clear that the Head Teachers do not want to play the role of Chief Executive. They want to be part of the educational and pastoral care and development of their children.

For this debate, the redoubtable Dame Mavis Grant spoke to air some of these worries. Getting someone to speak in favour of the changes was more difficult. In the end it went slightly askew. I was recommended Professor James Tooley from the School of Education at Newcastle University. James is an acknowledged expert in schools run entirely by the private sector. We had advertised a debate about school Governors but James wanted to talk more broadly about school governance. A number of the audience were strongly ideologically opposed to his point of view and were not expecting it to be put forward. James's ideas were very interesting, particularly his experiences of developing educational resources in India in areas where the state systems are failing badly and private run systems are succeeding. He got a hard time from the audience and left a little unhappy.

I said it earlier and I'll say it again: we will get education on a par with the best in Europe when we put in as much money as they do. All the fancy theories in the world are no substitute for resources.

The 'Environment' debate was packed. This was not surprising, as the venue is only half a mile away from the Byker incinerator plant that had hit the national headlines earlier in the year in a pollution scandal. The major problem was that ash from the plant was used to spread on paths on allotments throughout the city. This ash contained levels of heavy metals and dioxins in a concentration unheard of before. This came about because clinker ash, that's the stuff that falls through the grate at the bottom, was mixed with fly ash, that's the stuff that sticks to the side of the chimney. The clinker ash is relatively inert and safe but the fly ash is highly toxic and modern scientific advice and current good practice should have separated them. A strong local campaign had sprung up around this issue fuelled, pardon the pun, by a strong belief amongst environmental campaigners that incineration was a lazy if not dangerous approach to waste disposal and that only strong policies on re-cycling would deal with this issue in the long term.

Re-cycling was certainly a major theme of the debate and the country generally was lambasted for its poor and inadequate approach to developing strong policies on the issue. Once again the global perspective was evident. Poor and third world countries re-cycle just about anything because it has value within their economies. In rich countries re-cycling is difficult because it is cheaper to throw things away. One of the reasons we Councillors had been constantly given for slow progress in re-cycling was the cost. Public money is a precious resource and we are supposed to use it as efficiently as possible. Could we justify spending quite a lot more on waste disposal by re-cycling and what other services should be cut back to pay for it? It emerged during the debate that one reason that paper re-cycling was uneconomic in Britain was because of Germany. Germany is often held up as an example of good practice. If you have ever been there you may well have noticed that every household and business uses several bins. Paper, plastics and glass are all separated at source, which is good re-cycling practice. However the Germans had been storing vast quantities of paper in warehouses and a few years ago simply dumped it on the European market at rock-bottom prices. Thus the price of re-cycled paper was hugely uneconomic for British Local Authorities. It's that Einstein quote again: as soon as we tug one strand…

'Elected Mayors' is another ideological obsession of the Government and the debate was good fun. At the end both our speakers: Sir Jeremy Beecham (Chair of the Local Government Association as well as Councillor for Benwell, the neighbouring ward to Elswick), and Nigel Todd (my fellow Elswick Councillor and a leading advocate for elected Mayors) kind of agreed with each other. What matters are the policies and principles a Local Authority holds and carries out. The structure of how they do it – Committees, Cabinets or Mayors – are only the form through which the content is delivered.

We had a great panel for the Health debate with Rita Stringfellow, the Local Government Association spokeswoman on Health and Social Services and Leader of neighbouring North Tyneside Council, a current Chief Executive of a Health Trust, and a recently retired one, a homeopath, a disability activist and Liam Donaldson the Chief Medical Officer for the Government. Liam, incidentally, is an example of the fanaticism of Newcastle United fans, still a season ticket holder from the days when he worked in the region he now often takes a day return from Kings Cross to watch the team.

Snippets from this debate included an admission from all the panel members that they had used alternative or complementary medicine at some time in their lives and were perfectly comfortable with that. I even recall that there was a tacit acceptance that the legalisation of cannabis would not be a terrible disaster for the nation. There was also an important agreement that too much weight has been given in the past to academically based healthcare professional training and that a more practically based approach was a more useful contemporary tool. My friend Dr Anand, who wasn't part of this debate unfortunately, sums this up very well. The trouble with Doctors, he asserts, is that they are only experts in illness, they know next to nothing about health.

The last two debates took place in May during the final days of my year in office. There is a very strong campaign in the North-East in favour of regional government. We perceive ourselves seriously disadvantaged by our distance from the centre of power in Britain and by the whole 'London is the centre of the universe' syndrome. Support goes pretty much across the board including the Labour and Liberal Democrat parties, and much of business. There are people in both those parties and quite a few in business, of course, who do not support it; but it does have an unusual cross-section of the community in its favour. The only grouping in solid opposition is the Conservative Party. I was keen to get a business representative to speak in favour and a Conservative to oppose.

The first was easy. Bill Midgley is an ex-Chief Executive of Newcastle Building Society, an immediate past president of the North East Chamber of Commerce and currently Chairman of Durham County Cricket Club. He is also vice-chair of the North East Regional Assembly, the half-hearted shadow advisory body the Government has allowed to be set up. I hinted earlier in the book that Conservatives are becoming a rare breed in the region and it took a little time for someone to agree to speak against, but in the end we got an excellent speaker, Karl Poulson, who was the Conservative parliamentary candidate in Tynemouth. I was really unsure how the argument against Regional Government would be assembled but Karl did it very well. I did not agree with him at all but I concede he made an excellent fist of it. Bill, too, was an excellent advocate for his view and a cracking debate ensued. In some ways the conclusion was similar to that of the elected Mayor debate. It's not necessarily the structure of governance or government that will make a difference to the region but the content of the policies pursued by the representatives within that structure.

Finally we came to a subject dear and close to my heart, Arts and Culture. In the past ten years the region has gradually developed one of the most exciting and dynamic infrastructures in the United Kingdom. It is exciting because of the balanced approach, which has been nurtured by some exceptional individuals and organisations. Of course there is some total crap too, some of it from large and well funded cultural groups, but that has always been the case. What excites me is the recognition that all communities have a right to relevant and accessible activities. I talked much earlier about my experiences in the late 1970s with Bruvvers, pioneering new styles of theatre work designed for new audiences. A number of organisations and individuals in the region have held on to the principles of those days and now find themselves, finally, much more in tune with a broader band of thought on culture. In some ways their time has arrived. That is why I am not just an enthusiastic supporter of the bid by Newcastle and Gateshead to become European Capital of Culture in 2008, I think we are going to win it.

The panel were fantastic and the debate stimulating, the only problem was that the recording of it all failed to work. That's technology for you. Trying to pin down what we mean by Arts and Culture is a slippery fish. Our culture is everything about the way we live our lives; our beliefs, attitudes, traditions, loyalties, social interactions, and so on. Health, wealth, welfare and happiness all depend upon it. Culture is, to use a currently fashionable phrase, central to social inclusion.

There is still a long way to go in gaining a proper understanding of these issues amongst our leaders and decision-makers. In a recent professorial lecture at the University of Northumbria – 'For Better, For Worse? What Future For The North East' – Dr Fred Robinson, who was on our Money and Debt panel, made some telling comments on the current set up within government agencies and policies in the region. The Regional Economic Strategy, developed by these Agencies has an impressive overall vision:

'By 2010, the North East is a vibrant, self-reliant and outward looking region with the aspiration, ambition and confidence to unlock the potential of all its people.'

Unfortunately it then goes on to define a pecking order. Top of the list is economic growth, with social inclusion in second place. Wrong, wrong, wrong! They must be seen as equal partners. Economic growth before social inclusion will always ensure the needs of business are met before the needs of the community, the people. Business is global, and its needs do not conform to the needs of the communities who provide the labour and skills which feed it. A global culture is a culture of Capital not Communities. We should celebrate and nurture diversity.

To make matters worse, economic growth is the responsibility of the Regional Development Agency, One North East, whilst social inclusion and culture are the responsibility of an entirely separate agency, the Government Office for the North East. Joined up government – mon derrière. As I write there are six years and another general election to go before 2008, so there is time. I hope to see the Capital of Culture on Tyneside not the Culture of Capital

The whole theme of the debates and Agenda 21 was to demonstrate how essential it is to start to take more control over our affairs, not continue the drift towards national and international dominance of them.

Clare and I would like sincerely to thank every person who took part in, and helped to make happen, the 21 Debates. It was fun, it was illuminating, and I hope the spirit of what we tried to stimulate carries on forever.

And finally

Well it was a great time, a great year. Like anything else it had its ups and downs but having decided I was going to go for it, despite some major reservations about what the whole thing symbolised, I had to give it my best shot. According to the office I had a total, of 551 engagements, an average of one and a half engagements every single day! Most of the time we managed to have fun and find pleasure in what we did. On one occasion we even managed to turn what could have been an embarrassing *faux pas* into an amusing incident.

I have one or two unappealing habits. Yes just one or two! I have already confessed how easy it is to overdo the alcohol and I did, once or twice. Alcohol of course is a seriously debilitating and expensive drug addiction within our society. Millions of working days are lost through excessive consumption and millions, if not a billion or two, is spent by the National Health Service on repairing the damage it does to us. The social, medical and economic cost, I suspect, probably outweighs the tax take.

The other drug I must confess to enjoying is tobacco. I roll my own. Nicotine is, I believe, the most addictive drug known. In today's official no smoking climate it can be quite difficult to indulge. The Civic Centre, head office of the Council, is entirely no smoking and I was always having to nip out for a quick one. One afternoon this all went horribly wrong.

I was engaged on a busy schedule of visits that day and I became increasingly desperate so, breaking the rules, I lit up in the back of the Mayoral Limousine. As I knew I was being naughty I opened the window wide to minimise the pollution inside the car. Unfortunately in my haste I had not rolled a very tight tube and the wind caught a loose fragment of burning tobacco and hurled it against the seat back. I did not notice at the time but soon had it pointed out to me by a somewhat disgruntled driver. The hole was approximately the size of half a drawing pin head. I thought no more about it although I resolved never to do it again. However, even a tiny blemish like that is regarded as despoiling the appearance of the Limo so it had to get fixed. Someone in the Lord Mayor's Office – and I have my suspicions – leaked the story and the next thing I knew it was a big picture article in the local evening paper. Naturally, even at that early stage, half the facts in the article were wrong, but you come to accept the journalistic rubric that one should never let the facts get in the way of a good story. Next thing I know the *Sun* newspaper has picked up the story which it titled, quite brilliantly, 'It's Alight Mayor' (nightmare – get it?). Not one to be outdone I then told everyone who asked about it that the whole

thing was a cover up story. In fact, I claimed, I had tried to torch the whole Limo as a protest against global capitalism.

A couple of days after the *Sun* headline I was quietly pottering in my back garden when the phone rang. And who was on the other end but The Big Breakfast Show. 'Mr Mayor we want you to come down to London to the studio tomorrow, you have won the Big Breakfast pun of the week'. Well it wos the *Sun* wot won it and I, fortunately I suspect, had official engagements which made it impossible to go.

There are lots of fond memories. I operated a JCB and dug a hole in the ground. I opened the Smoothe Wrap café run by an old friend, Debbie, who, with her partner, has demonstrated that resourcefulness Geordies are so full of by bringing a new catering idea into the Toon. I watched Tony Blair be cleverly coaxed into playing the guitar by some musicians when he came to visit the new Northern Arts premises. I saw a marvellous stained glass window consecrated, celebrating the bravery of seamen and others in the defence of the island of Malta. I was able to welcome the Secretary of State for Health to a conference on Arts and Health, the area of work I had become so involved in through South Tyneside Arts Studio.

I was given the opportunity by The Grand Union Orchestra to play my soprano saxophone in front of a packed audience at the Newcastle Playhouse, backed by eight of the best jazz musicians in the country. That was a wonderful thrill. In fact someone came up to me a month or so after that gig and told me he assumed I was miming at first but, he said, 'You really can play'. Oh how my heart swelled. I told you at the beginning how susceptible to flattery I was. Actually I really can play. I have done for 25 years. I fact I have the proud distinction of being the last person successfully prosecuted for busking in Newcastle ... but that was 20 years ago ...

I met some heroes too. Alan Shearer was not a bad start but there were others, including two Trade Unionists, whom I was especially proud to have received. Jack Jones was leader of the

Transport and General Workers before retiring and taking up the cudgels on behalf of Britain's pensioners. Jack came to the city to officiate at the opening of a new regional headquarters of ACAS, the Arbitration, Conciliation and Advisory Service, which works on behalf of good labour and industrial relationships. Well into his 80s, he was as bright as a button and his commitment to the poor and disadvantaged within our society was clearly undimmed.

The other was Rodney Bickerstaff who retired early in 2001 as leader of Unison, the public services union. Rodney has been an uncompromising fighter for his members who have, over the past 15 years, been subjected to huge pressures for reform and change. I believe in public services as a vital part of our national culture; I also recognise that they must continually adapt and evolve and Rodney has shown great leadership in this process. We gave him a dinner as he had long standing connections with the city and I got the opportunity to start at least one speech at the Mansion House with the words 'Comrades, Brothers and Sisters'. Such phrases are nostalgic these days but they had a meaning for me that night and, I hope, for others. Funnily enough, on his retirement from Unison, Rodney was to pick up the mantle from Jack Jones in leading the pensioners' organisation so there is a neat tie up. They will be in good hands.

There were many other occasions when I met heroic people, people who had distinguished themselves in some way within the city. Often I felt very humble in the face of their dedication and achievements. So much unsung heroism goes on in our society, and I feel privileged to have been able to thank them on behalf of the community.

I will remember my year with great affection but I cannot close without a word of advice to Bobby Robson, and all future managers of Newcastle United. Remember the motto of the city: 'Fortiter Triumphans Defendit' – A strong defence will triumph.

Howay the Toon!

Appendix

Agenda 21 - what it's all about

We came up with two parallel sets of three descriptions. The first was Environment, Social and Economic; the second Equity, Participation and Futurity.

ENVIRONMENT

• Do we use energy, water and other natural resources efficiently and with care?
• How do we minimise waste, and then re-use or recover it through re-cycling, composting, or energy recovery and then finally dispose of what is left sustainably?
• How can we limit pollution to levels that do not damage natural systems?
• How can we value and protect the diversity of nature?

SOCIAL

• We need to create or enhance places, spaces and buildings that work well, wear well and look well.
• We should make settlements human in scale and form.
• We must value and protect diversity and local distinctiveness, and strengthen local community and cultural identity.
• Protection of human health and amenity through safe, clean and pleasant environments.
• Emphasise health service preventative action, as well as care.
• Ensure access to good food, water, housing and fuel, at a reasonable cost.

• Meeting local needs locally; wherever possible.
• Maximise everyone's access to skills and knowledge needed to play a full part in society.
• Empower all sections of the community to participate in decision making and consider the social and community impact of decisions.

ECONOMIC
• Creating a vibrant local economy that gives access to satisfying and rewarding work without damaging the local or global environment.
• Value unpaid work.
• Encourage necessary access to facilities, services, goods and other people in ways which make less use of cars, and minimise impact on the environment.
• Make opportunities for culture, leisure, and recreation available to all.

~

EQUITY
• Are resources and benefits provided equally?
• Is the quality of services improved in an equitable manner?
• Is the quality of life improved?

PARTICIPATION
• Do the means allow and encourage people to shape the decisions that will affect them?
• Do people have an equal access to decision making?
• Is decision making made more understandable and open to scrutiny?
• Do decision makers carry responsibility for, and feel the effects of, their decisions?

FUTURITY

- Do the decisions make the best use of resources: money, materials, the environment and people's skills?
- Are decisions based upon a long term view?
- Will the benefits last?
- Will our children and grandchildren approve of the decisions?
- Do the proposals encourage an integration of policies?